TENDER ESCAPE

"It was a lovely evening, thank you." Olivia looked as if she were about to extend a hand for a shake.

"Don't thank me," Clifton said, leaning against the wooden surface, regarding her. "This is officially our second date." He stepped closer to her, grasped her hand, and pulled her to him, giving her plenty of time to pull back if she wanted to. "This means a good-night kiss."

She didn't pull back, but lifted her face to him. "Oh yeah?"

He smiled. "Must have been that floppy hat, or those shades, or your softness, that took my breath away." His voice caught with the last syllable. He lowered his head.

"I've wanted to taste your lips since we met at that restaurant," he whispered.

"Then what are you waiting for?"

The smile left his eyes, replaced by unmistakable desire. Thrusting his tongue between her lips, he deepened the kiss.

She tasted like sweet ambrosia. Their tongues volleyed. He could taste her forever. The teaser had only whetted his appetite. He wanted more of her—to touch her all over.

ALSO BY CANDICE POARCH

INTIMATE SECRETS
THE ESSENCE OF LOVE
WITH THIS KISS
WHITE LIGHTNING
"More Than Friends"
in **A MOTHER'S TOUCH**
"A New Year, A New Beginning"
in **MOONLIGHT & MISTLETOE**

Published by BET/Arabesque books

TENDER ESCAPE

Candice Poarch

BET Publications, LLC
www.msbet.com
www.arabesquebooks.com

ACKNOWLEDGMENTS TO:

The many people who helped with the research I needed for this novel. Thank you.
Deborah Aylward for her patience in answering many questions on investigative procedures.
Connie Rosenthal for her help on facials and therapeutic massages.
Joyce Weber, Jerry O'Neil, Marta Goldblatt, Yvette Holly, David Nutile, and Neville Withington.
Sandy Rangel, my critique partner. This is your year.

ARABESQUE BOOKS are published by

BET Publications, LLC
c/o BET BOOKS
One BET Plaza
1900 W Place NE
Washington, D.C. 20018-1211

First Printing: February, 2000

10 9 8 7 6 5 4 3 2 1
Printed in the United States of America

Prologue

Slugger gazed at Dad's picture carefully nestled in a silver-plated frame. They had done such fun things together. When Slugger was little, they'd gone together to collect his gambling winnings or—when Dad had run short of money and had begged and borrowed the money—to return to make the payoff. Slugger even knew where he went to gamble. Trouble was, Dad didn't know when to stop, and he never held on to his winnings very long.

He was dead. Twelve long years ago. The pang should be far less intense by now. It wasn't. Slugger's hand pressed a queasy stomach. The agony of missing Dad struck like a dagger, shredding the insides to ribbons.

All the fun went out of Slugger's life the moment he died.

Slugger loved Mom, but a more serious woman

never crossed the path of Prince Georges County—
besides Olivia, that is. It was work, work, work, all the
time. *Do your homework. Clean your room.* Never walks
along the Potomac, or bicycle rides in Rock Creek
Park. And Mom worked herself nearly to death with
two full-time jobs—a secretary during the day, security guard at night.

Oh God, how Slugger had loved riding with Dad
on Saturday mornings while Mom was catching up
on her sleep from the long work week. On Friday
nights Slugger stayed with Grandma, and wakened
to Dad's booming laughter. The two of them sneaked
out together. Never on Sunday, because Mom insisted
on Sunday School and church.

Grandma always said if Dad didn't straighten up
she'd stop him from coming around. It had been an
empty threat, and they both knew it. Dad always had
that special place in Grandma's heart. She always said
he could charm the birds from the trees.

If it wasn't for the fact that Mom had to rely on
Dad's mother to keep Slugger, Slugger would have
hardly gotten to see Dad at all. And as much as Dad
wanted it, craved it, begged for it, Mom never married
him. Too unstable, she'd said. Unreliable.

Slugger stroked a lean hand across his likeness,
smiling back. "*Oh, Daddy,*" Slugger whispered tear-
fully. "Why did you do it? We didn't need the money.
I needed *you.*" Slugger and Dad had shared secrets—
lots of secrets—that Slugger still clutched close to
the heart.

Slugger's attention was directed to the pitiful paycheck laying on the table, and thoughts of the future.
Mom had begged Slugger to go to college. *You can*

be a doctor, a teacher, a scientist, or a businessperson. You're so smart. Use it. You can be anything, if only you go to college, Mom said.

Eager to start working to bring in a paycheck, that wasn't an option. Slugger had gone without so much as a child because they couldn't afford much—especially after Mom bought the townhouse. She'd been so proud, then, but they were flat broke after the mortgage payment and bills.

Putting off college for later made Mom beg, "Don't pattern yourself after your father." But like father, like child. He lived on. Inside.

Finding his murderer was the goal. And now Slugger would find him. The only drawback was that after spending long days at the pitiful job—which was barely enough to pay the bills and a little extra—little time was left over to search for his killer.

A nice reward awaited anyone who chanced upon the location of that money. Anyone could live a long time off that reward money—even apply for college, a move that would please Mom immensely. That money could make life a heck of a lot easier for Mom. And it would be a reward, not stolen—Mom would never take stolen money. She deserved it. Daddy had died, and the person who convinced him to participate in the robbery was still out there, living the rich life, if not famous.

The goal was to see to it that he'd soon be famous, but not rich. Twelve years was a long time to wait for justice. Slugger wouldn't wait any longer.

Chapter 1

Twelve years ago

Olivia Hammond faced three high school friends, her grief hanging over her like a dense cloud.

Friends, she thought. She and Debra had been friends since third grade, when Debra had moved two doors down from her in Regency Apartments in Southeast, DC. Diane and Tonya had become friends with them through the high school drama club, when they'd performed together.

They'd gone to movies together, summer camp, church, and even hung out at the prom with their dates together. She wondered if the four of them could work together once again.

Boneless from her loss, Olivia only wanted to lie in her bed and give in to her grief. But she couldn't.

She had two small children, seven and five, who depended on her.

One hour at a time, she thought, and glanced at the pitcher of Kool-Aid and plate of sugar cookies on the scarred cocktail table she and Joe had brought at a garage sale for a song a month and a half ago. They'd planned to sand and refinish it to highlight the natural grain of the wood. Olivia crossed her arms below her breasts, clutching her elbows with each hand.

Joe was dead, killed in a senseless hit-and-run accident. Was it already a month ago? She clutched her elbows tighter and turned her back to her guests, thankful they were engrossed in their own conversations, as a tear escaped her lids. How many times had she told herself she'd shed her last tear . . . that there couldn't be a drop of moisture left in her? And every time she'd proved herself wrong. Even now, when she felt weak in the knees and split in two, she tried to use Joe's strength to keep her upright. Drying her tears with the back of her hand, she searched for something to do. The more active she stayed, the more able she was to cope. Activity left less time to think and mope.

The cookies and punch needed replenishing, she remembered, focusing on the mundane task. Locking her knees, she swiveled to face the table. Taking the plate and bowl in each hand, she started for the kitchen.

Debra appeared at her side, relieving her of the punch bowl, and fell in step beside her. Debra's shoes clicked rhythmically on the scarred hardwood floors. *Olivia hasn't had time to buy throw rugs or sand the floor yet*, she thought as she opened the peeling door to the kitchen.

Debra was a friend of few words, but she chattered incessantly now as she filled the plate with cookies and mixed up another batch of Kool-Aid in the bowl while Olivia gathered strength, tuning out the one-sided discourse. Her friend had been her anchor the last few weeks, helping her with funeral arrangements, forcing her to eat, helping out with the children. Before she knew it, Debra was marching through the swinging doors back to the living room.

Glancing around, Olivia inhaled a huge breath, seized the plate of cookies from the table, and followed her.

Sitting on the old ragged couch Olivia had covered with an inexpensive spread, Diane placed her eight-month-old on her shoulder, stroking the child's back. She leaned over and took a cookie. "These are really good," she said, biting into the treat.

Olivia merely smiled and sat in a chair across from the cocktail table. The springs squealed in protest. She also reached for a cookie, then checked herself when she remembered how Joe had hated the extra pounds she'd gained after her second pregnancy. She'd blown up, and hadn't been able to lose the weight. She straightened in her seat. She really didn't want the cookie, anyway. She hadn't tasted anything people had shoved at her for the last few weeks.

Tonya, who had been Olivia's friend since ninth grade, swallowed the Kool-Aid and nodded. "The punch, too." Then she suddenly set the glass on a wooden coaster Olivia had bought at a yard sale, seeming to be as weary of pretending as Olivia was.

"How are you and the kids doing, girl?" she said. "It was such a shock. Joe was a good man.

"It always happens to the good ones. He drove all that money from place to place every day in that armored truck, and he's done in by a hit-and-run car," Tonya added. She left her seat and moved next to Olivia to pat her hand, offering comfort. She sat on the arm of Olivia's chair and put an arm around her shoulder.

Olivia tried her best not to burst into tears again, but it wasn't easy. "We're okay," she stammered. She wasn't, really, but that was what people expected to hear—wanted to hear—even friends. They didn't quite know what to do to console, beyond the weak offers of help and compassionate words that escaped her when she was alone—in the dead of night, when she realized that she had two young children to provide for . . . now without a husband, without enough insurance money left over after burying Joe to pay even three months of the new mortgage. They'd moved into their fixer-upper on Georgia Avenue only two months ago. How happy they'd been. Both of them had grown up in apartments, and they'd longed to be homeowners.

Joe had loved this house. He'd seen more potential in it than even she could. But Olivia knew she couldn't dwell on that any longer. She had to find some means of supporting her children, and of keeping this house that meant so much to him. The time to get down to business had arrived.

"At least he put you in a decent home," Diane said.

Olivia nodded and cleared her throat.

Tonya returned to the couch.

"Actually," Olivia said. "That's why Debra and I called you all here. I have to find a job. I've finished two and a half years of college, but I have a year and a half to go. If I get a regular job, day care will take up a huge portion of my check. I've heard some of you complain about how dissatisfied you are with your jobs."

"You can say that again," Diane said, nodding her head and patting her baby's back. "I don't make enough to live alone, even with my mom taking care of Alonzo. If she charged me, I couldn't afford to work. I pay her something, but it's not enough."

"Well, I thought that maybe we could start a cleaning business together. Just until we can take some college courses or learn trades that will make us more employable."

"The economy's better," Debra added from across the room. She sat in a ladder-back chair near the fireplace. "More and more women have jobs."

"And the wages for domestic help are higher than they used to be. I've done some research. There are commercial contracts, which pay more and take less time. If we decide to do this, I know of two buildings that are open for bids right now. So we'd have to move quickly. They aren't large, but it's a start."

"The problem is day care," Tonya said. "I have two children. Who's going to take care of them while I'm making minimum wage?"

Tonya was in the same boat as Olivia, with two young children and no child support, except that her husband had left her.

"Debra's moving in here to cut down on rent. My

basement is large enough for you and your two children. With the three families living here, I could afford my mortgage, and that would give you someplace to live.''

Tonya looked askance at the peeling paint, scruffed floors, and dilapidated furniture.

Olivia and Joe had lived with yard sale specials while they'd saved for the down payment for the house. Olivia had planned for her high school graduation and wedding at the same time. Less than a month after she graduated, they were married. A year later their first child was born. Olivia had never worked outside the home.

''We can work together to paint and make some minor repairs,'' Olivia added hopefully.

''She's willing to let us use the extra room on this floor as an office, and the big family room in the basement as a day-care center.'' Debra pulled the ladder-back chair she occupied from the corner to sit beside Olivia.

''My mom will be happy to help with day care,'' Diane said. ''She's good with children. And her social security doesn't pay nearly enough to live off of.''

''If she's willing to commit, she can get someone to work with her, and maybe take in a few more children. I know some of the neighbors are looking for reliable day care.''

As the conversation continued agreeably, the fist that had clutched Olivia's chest for the last two weeks eased a bit. Maybe the plan she and Debra had cooked up would work, after all, she thought as the conversation swirled around her.

''The rest of us could run the cleaning business.

Make up flyers and leave them on the doors in the suburbs. On bulletin boards in grocery stores," Debra said.

"My sister can help out, too. She loves kids, and hates her job. She's making minimum wage right now," Tonya said.

"Two of my sisters are willing to help with the cleaning," Debra said. "I forgot to tell you that they want to return to school." Then she glanced at the ladies on the couch. "Let's take a few days to think about it. Before they quit their jobs, we'll see how much business we can drum up. In the meantime, Debra and I can draw up some notes and work on the contracts for those buildings."

Chapter 2

Present Day

Olivia wrapped her hand around the elegant brass doorknob of the Peacock Restaurant. She flexed her fingers and pulled the heavy wooden object open. Adjusting the strap of the leather bag swinging from her left shoulder, she glided into the dim structure, the thick carpeting muting her footsteps.

She was running out of time.

She advanced into a room of tables covered with white linen cloths and decorated with stylishly fashioned pink napkins.

Olivia stood near the door for a few seconds, letting her eyes adjust to the darkness made worse by the dark shades she wore for anonymity.

"A table for one?" The modulated tone of a host dressed in a tuxedo-like jacket with black trousers barely registered above the low buzz of conversations in the background. Perhaps lunchtime wasn't the best time to dine anonymously, since a slew of people were in the vicinity on business lunches.

"No, I'm meeting someone . . ." Olivia stopped when a tall man approached her and extended a hand.

As his larger hand enveloped Olivia's smaller one, she was struck by his gorgeous eyes—hazel, or some might refer to them as honey.

He had a nice clean scent about him, with just a hint of cologne.

"I'm Olivia Hammond," she said.

"Clifton Zayne."

During the greeting she looked for similarities between him and his sister, Veronica, who frequented The Total Woman, Olivia's day spa, located in Prince Georges County.

"I've heard a lot about your spa. It's quite popular." With a gentle hand at the crook of her elbow, Clifton guided her to a table for two where menus were already placed at each setting.

As Olivia settled into the chair he held for her, she glanced briefly at him again to assure herself that his eyes really were hazel. His complexion was only slightly darker than her own medium brown one, but his eyes were very different. His close-clipped haircut clearly delineated a strong jawbone. His bronze-toned mustache covered a sensuous upper lip.

A tinge of ruggedness in his appearance enhanced his looks, and Olivia's heart slammed against her chest. *Get a grip,* she admonished. *This is a business meeting.* But he was such an unexpected shock. She'd expected a stone-faced, shortish man, since he'd been a cop for several years, and Veronica couldn't be more than five-three. But he stood at least six-one, quite tall, forbidding, and darn fine.

The smattering of gray sprinkled along his temples only enhanced his appearance. A starched white shirt pressed against his well-built chest. Olivia stifled a regrettable sigh. *He probably prefers his women toned and thin,* she thought. He wasn't overly muscled, just detailed enough for her to sense that he worked out on a regular basis. He certainly wouldn't be attracted to a more than slightly overweight woman.

Olivia had tried for years, but still couldn't resist chocolate cakes, butter pecan ice cream, and ribs smothered in southern barbecue sauce.

An efficient waitress wearing a ruffled white blouse and black skirt appeared at their table, introduced herself, took their drink orders of ice tea, and departed as silently as she'd approached.

"How may I help you, Ms. Hammond?" Clifton asked, moving his menu aside.

Forcing her attention from him to the purpose of the luncheon, Olivia noticed a small, black spiral notebook on the table beside his napkin. A blue Bic pen lay across the binder.

"I'm being blackmailed," she whispered, sliding her purse between the chair and the table leg. She glanced around the room, then refocused on him. How did one handle these affairs? She'd never dealt with a private investigator before.

"Have you contacted the police?" he asked.

"No, I haven't."

"Why not?"

"I know it wasn't a wise move, but when he contacted me I paid him five thousand. I don't know how I made myself believe that would be the only time he'd ask."

"Has he asked for more?"

"No."

He opened the notebook and began to scribble. "When did he contact you?"

"Four weeks ago." She'd hoped it would all go away, but just as she couldn't close her eyes to Uncle Sam, neither could she ignore a blackmailer. Olivia felt more and more uncomfortable as each minute passed. Repeating the tale made her feel silly for paying the money in the first place. Even teenagers knew better than to pay blackmailers. But she'd had only a short period of time to act.

"How did he contact you?" he asked.

"I received a letter in the mail." Needing to do something with her hands, she smoothed the napkin in her lap.

"At home, or at the spa?"

"At home." She frowned. "Is that important?"

"Could be. I imagine you didn't recognize his voice."

"The voice was disguised."

"But definitely male?"

Olivia shook her head no.

"So why did you refer to the blackmailer as he?"

Olivia had just assumed . . . "I don't know, really."

Clifton nodded and made a notation on his pad.

"Blackmailers usually repeat requests for more money when they run out. It's also illegal to pay one."

"I didn't know that."

"What does someone have that's valuable enough for you to pay that much money to keep it quiet?"

She threw him a startled look before she could stifle it. "It's a long story," she finally said.

Clifton wondered if the distinguished woman before him had indulged in some hot, illicit affair. Buttoned down tighter than a nun, she epitomized graciousness and elegance, and reminded him of some of his teachers—he'd thought they would never let a man touch them. Even those with children, he'd thought as a child, had conceived through immaculate conception.

Putting the pen on the table, he leaned back in his chair. "I've got all afternoon."

Olivia took a deep breath. "Twelve years ago," she said, shifting in her seat, "the armored truck that my husband drove was highjacked. The robbers got away with millions of dollars worth of gold bricks."

"How many millions?"

"Fifteen or twenty, I believe."

He expelled an inaudible whistle. "Was any recovered?"

"Not that I'm aware of. Right after the robbery they questioned everyone—the drivers, anyone who worked there, those who worked especially in that division. Then, two weeks later, my husband was killed in a hit-and-run accident."

"Did they find the driver?"

"No. It was on a dark street at night." Oh, Lord, it had been such a nightmare. Olivia closed her eyes and rubbed her temple.

She felt a warm hand cover hers, and opened her eyes.

"Take your time," Clifton said softly.

She nodded and continued. "Afterward, they questioned me. Asked me if he had done anything strange lately, seen any unusual people, or strayed from his usual pattern. Sometimes it felt like someone was following me. Eventually the scrutiny died down, but I was left with the impression that they believed it was an inside job. They never discovered who planned it, and they never recovered the money. But my Joe was *not* involved. That much I know. Joe was the most honest person I've ever known." Her mouth trembled on the last word.

"*Had* he done anything unusual? Phone calls, trips?"

"No," she said quickly. Too quickly.

He regarded her for a moment. She was unable to read his expression. "So, what happened recently?"

"I received copies of clippings about the robbery in the mail, and about Joe's death. The letter said they can tie Joe to the robbery, that he was part of it, and the blackmailer believes I'm living off the money." She tried to keep anger from seeping into her voice, but she couldn't. "I worked myself to the bone those first few years to make ends meet. Some friends of mine and I started a cleaning business, and we scrubbed kitchens and bathrooms during the day and went to night school." She sipped on her tea and slowly set the frosted glass on the table. Her eyes met his with serious intent. "I didn't have an easy ride or any free money, and I'm not paying another penny to this blackmailer. With two children in college, I don't have it to throw away."

Clifton regarded the fiercely determined, full-figured woman across from him. Dressed in a stylish, dark gray business suit and a lavender blouse that served to enhance her soft beauty, she had yet to take off her oversize sunshades. He didn't know how she could see at all in the dimly lit interior. A wide-brimmed hat slanted to the side hid most of her face. Her short hair framed a lovely mocha face—at least what he could see of it. He could imagine that her eyes probably held the fierceness of a tigress who plainly projected that, come hell or high water, she'd take care of her own. Her emotions came through clearly, if not her visage.

Clifton wondered why she'd gone to all the trouble. The restaurant was thirty minutes from her home, and in the middle of nowhere. As soon as she'd entered the restaurant, the floppy hat, sunshades, expensive black purse—a cross between a briefcase and handbag, made of high-quality leather by a top designer—all drew attention to her, and only served to make her more noticeable.

The door opened and she glanced at it, her hands tensing on the table—delicate, rose-painted nails, no hangnails, no ragged cuticles, and a plain, inexpensive gold band on her right hand.

She sat in view of the door and every time it opened she glanced in that direction.

"Relax," he said. "If anyone sees us, they'll think we're on a date or out for an illicit affair."

He'd meant the facetious statement to calm her, but her startled look and the warmth in her cheeks enchanted him. It shouldn't have.

"Tell me more about the heist," he said.

"I've told you everything I know. Most of the information I gathered from the news, just like everyone else, except for the questioning. I wasn't any help because I didn't know anything. I can tell you that, as far as anyone knows, all the robbers were eventually killed—one died a month later in gunfire. By the time he died, the gold was hidden without a trace."

"May I see the letter?"

Reaching beside her, she opened her purse, extracted the envelope and handed the mangled object across the small table.

Clifton took the envelope and shook out a regular letter-size sheet of white paper and opened it with his pen. The blackmailer had used a low-grade ink jet printer. And the postage stamp was from the post office in PG County.

"Are you ready to order now?" the waitress asked.

Olivia jumped like a scalded cat.

"What would you like?" Closing the letter, Clifton opened his menu and scanned the lunch items.

Olivia snapped open her menu with a quick flick of her wrist. "What's your soup of the day?" she asked the waitress, who was hovering at her side.

"Cream of mushroom."

"I'll have the soup and half a tuna sandwich. In the meantime, please bring hot tea with lemon."

"Ditto for me," Clifton said, "Without the tea."

When the waitress left, Clifton turned his water glass round and round as he said slowly, "You know, this is something the police can handle. You should go to them."

"It wouldn't prove my husband's innocence. I want this settled once and for all. I'm willing to pay you for it. Tell me you'll take this case."

"I'm not saying I . . ." Clifton grew quiet as the waitress put the hot water and tea bag on the table in front of Olivia and quickly left.

"I brought everything with me." Olivia pulled a large manila envelope out of the bag. "Newspaper articles on the robbery, a picture of my husband and the men. There are seven employees in the picture, which was taken during a company picnic. I circled the four who were on the truck. I have Joe's social security number here. I don't have the others. Here's the name of the officer in charge of the case, as well as what I remembered about that time. I've saved everything."

Clifton took the proffered envelope and opened it, pulling out sheets of paper. As he scanned them, he was amazed at how thorough she was, but then he hadn't really expected anything less from a woman who worked her way through college and then into her own successful spa business that catered to the movers and shakers of Prince Georges County.

A PI had to be careful that the person he was dealing with was mentally balanced and didn't have ulterior motives. He didn't detect a problem here—so far— though he couldn't read her eyes. As far as he could detect, she truly believed her husband was innocent. Her body language spelled determination, confidence, with just a little fear.

The hit-and-run was too close to the date of the heist for Clifton to put it down to coincidence. That bit of information didn't make the man guilty in his eyes, but left something to file in his notes.

He focused on Olivia as she stirred sugar and then squeezed lemon into her tea. Was her husband truly innocent, or was she one of those women who stood by her man even though he'd been dead for more than a decade?

Still, he wondered what she'd omitted. Clients always failed to divulge something, whether it was intentional or not.

"Look, Mrs. Hammond. I don't like to discourage business, but in a heist of that magnitude the police as well as investigators for the insurance company would have turned this case upside down to recover that money. After twelve years, the trail would be cold, and it could cost you more than that five thousand."

"The police don't have my best interests at heart. To them this blackmail attempt would only confirm what they already believe, that my husband was involved." She closed her eyes and rubbed her forehead. "Look, can't you at least try to find the person who's blackmailing me? That's a new lead, isn't it?" she asked hopefully. She reached for her overstuffed bag again and pulled out a checkbook and a gold Mont Blanc fountain pen. "Will a thousand-dollar retainer do?" Her pen hovered over the checkbook.

"You do realize I'd be investigating a twelve-year-old robbery? I wouldn't begin to work on a case of this magnitude with less than five thousand."

Her hand froze as she regarded him. "Five thousand . . . dollars?"

"Certainly not pesos. Just to be up front with you, I need to warn you that this case could cost as much as twenty thousand dollars with all the work that will be involved—with no guarantees. Our fee is seventy dollars an hour plus expenses."

Her mouth tightened. "Well, you certainly don't

need to commit robbery when you can do it legally to your clients, do you?" A saccharine smile barely escaped her tightened lips.

She scribbled furiously writing out the check, ripped it out, and handed it to him.

Clifton regarded her a moment, pulled out a contract from the breast pocket of his jacket, and handed it to her. If she wanted to spend money on this, he was willing to take it. In moments she handed him the signed document. He tucked both items in his breast pocket.

"At your rates, I'm sure you can afford to pay for lunch." She took her bag and slung the strap over her shoulder.

"I'll add it to expenses."

She set the purse on the table, fished out her Coach wallet. Taking out cash, she dropped it on her place setting.

"You can pay for your own." She barely gave Clifton a chance to make it out of his chair before she sailed by him.

Clifton trailed Olivia to her green Volvo and watched her pull into the traffic, blending with it. Not a flashy vehicle, but substantial—one made to last at least a decade. She valued quality. The suit she wore was made for endurance, and to enhance her looks. It accomplished both goals.

As Clifton opened the door of his black Taurus, he considered the five thousand. If the blackmailer really believed that Olivia had access to twenty million—or even a portion of it—the demand would have been for a heck of a lot more than five thousand, which left the search open to someone who merely wanted to steal money from Olivia. That would carry his search much wider than the people associated with the heist. It would include employees, neighbors, her children's friends.

Still, the heist was a good place to start, since she wanted the person who planned it found.

Clifton got into his black Taurus and backed out of the parking space. Olivia's checking account was with the Bank of Maryland. He drove by one of the branches and cashed the check. Olivia looked well off, but he'd had checks bounce before, and didn't work a case without up-front funds. A struggling PI couldn't afford to work a case just because he was attracted to the client.

With cash in hand, he drove by the window to Chesapeake Bank, where he and his partner had set up an account, and deposited the cash.

Then he returned to the office, where he set his sister Veronica on a database search for the families of the robbers. Olivia had obituaries of two of them who had been single.

There was nothing for Bailey, the robber who had been shot first, which meant a trip to the courthouse.

After an hour in the archives, Clifton discovered that Bailey had been married. He copied his wife's address in his notebook. Since her apartment was en route to his office, he headed to her high-rise apartment on Trailblazer Street.

Children were playing outside in the sandy area of swings and sawhorses. A group of men stood around a car, and one man's head was stuck under the hood, a dirty rag hanging from his pocket. The after-work crowd rushed into the building to cook their evening dinners.

Clifton entered the locked outer door with one of the occupants. It always mystified him that people paid extra for a secure building, yet let strangers slide in right behind them. He rode the elevator to the sixth floor. Stanley Bailey's wife lived in apartment 623. He smelled garlic and other spices in the hallway. The beige paint on the walls and doors was scarred and fading. He lifted a hand and rapped twice against the wooden surface. In a moment, he heard footsteps approaching.

A voice tinged with overly long use of cigarettes reached him through the paneling. "Yeah?"

"I'm looking for Joyce Bailey."

The chain rattled as a woman pulled the door open to the length of the safety chain. A partial view of thinning, dyed blond hair came into view through the crack.

"She don't live here any more. Passed on a few years back." She took a drag on her cigarette and blew the smoke away from the crack.

Down the hall on the opposite side, he heard a door open and—with his peripheral vision—watched a grayheaded woman peek through.

The woman sighed and rolled her eyes. "That nosy woman across the hall can tell you anything you want to know about her and her son. Nothing happens that she don't know about. They used to be close friends. I didn't know her."

"Thank you." Clifton filed the information about

the son and walked a few paces to the right. The door slammed as he approached it.

He knocked on the freshly painted surface. She probably bought her own paint and painted the door herself. The door opened immediately, to the same four-inch crack. Her short gray-streaked hair fell straight, limp and unstyled. The face was thin and wrinkled.

"I'm Clifton Zayne. I understand you knew Mrs. Bailey."

"What's it to you?"

"I've been hired to find her son. He's won some money in a sweepstakes, and they've been unable to deliver it to him for well over a year."

"Yeah?" The woman smiled, then shut the door in his face. He lifted his hand to knock again, then heard the chain rattling before it clattered against the structure. He dropped his hand to his side. This time she opened the door wide and stepped back to let him enter.

Clifton wondered if he'd been an investigator too long. He didn't let strangers in his house, and turned his back to them. He locked his house, his car doors. It always amazed him how people trusted anyone who said they were there to pay money, even to the point of letting strangers into their homes.

"I've got his address in here somewhere." She stood with her hand on a stack of magazines, contemplating. Neat little piles of books, magazines, and papers were stacked along the edge. He wondered where she ate, then glimpsed a lap table atop one of the sofa tables. She riffled through a pile of papers.

The television across the room blared "The Evening News with Maureen Bunyon."

The strong smell of vinegar that he'd whiffed since she opened the door grew stronger when he entered the large living room, dining room combination. The ceiling-to-floor drapes were pulled back, giving a view of the street and a small balcony with two white lawn chairs flanking a small round table.

"Here you go." She waved a piece of paper in her spotted hand.

Clifton took the pad and pen from his breast pocket and scribbled down the address and phone number.

"He and his wife used to call now and then, but I haven't heard from them in more than a year. Didn't even get a Christmas card last year," she lamented. "He's going to be happy about that money. You tell them 'hi' for me, you hear? And tell them don't be strangers."

"I will." Clifton handed the paper back to her, thanking her for the information, and left. He knew he should feel a twinge of guilt for lying, but it never bothered him to use the easiest route to information.

Once in the car, Clifton pulled out his map and looked up the address. In a few more months he'd know the area better, but for now the map would do. He saw that the Baileys' address should be no more than twenty minutes away, in Landover.

The traffic was beginning to thin as he pulled into the beltway traffic and made his way there. He drove through the townhouse section of the community until he found the address.

A harried woman carrying a child who looked to be no more than two answered the door. The child tangled her fingers in her mother's red curls as she reared back in full scream. The woman's face turned scarlet from pain, and the freckles across her face stood out in stark relief.

Frantically the woman untangled the fingers and told the child to be quiet.

The child gathered a huge breath—one like the ones Clifton's son took when he was really in a rage—but when she saw Clifton, she quieted instantly on a gulp.

"Yes?" the woman said in the blessed silence.

"I'm looking for Stanley Bailey."

"Good luck," she said as if she'd been glad to see the last of him. "Last I heard he was in California."

"I'm Clifton Zayne with the Peaceful Solutions Detective Agency. When will he be back?"

"Probably never. He up and left with his new girlfriend more than a year ago. What trouble is he in now? You about to garnish him or something?"

"We're investigating the armored heist that occurred twelve years ago."

"He's stayed away from out-and-out crime after what happened to his dad. We were neighbors, and it really threw him when his dad died."

"Do you remember anything about that heist?"

She shook her head as the little girl sucked on her thumb and watched Clifton. "I was only eleven at the time."

Clifton took out a card and handed it to her. "If you remember anything, give me a call."

"I don't think I'll be any help."

Clifton left and thought through his next move. Olivia hadn't given him very much to go on.

* * *

Olivia made her way back home and tugged out of her constricting clothing. Although it was September, the sweltering temperature lingered, and she was glad to rid herself of the suit and tight girdle. She knew many full-figured women did without tight undergarments, but she didn't believe in letting it all hang out. She expelled a breath. Breathing was a sight better without the constriction.

The question Clifton had asked about Joe's emotional state nagged at her. Of course he'd been edgy. Who wouldn't have been, after seeing the men— whose children had played with his own only a week ago at a company picnic—torn apart from the explosive impact of a submachine gun? But if she'd told the PI that, she was sure he would have immediately assumed the worst.

She was paying him—a freaking fortune, at that— for an unbiased investigation, and with the knowledge that her husband was innocent. Telling him Joe's actual state of mind would immediately prejudice him against her husband. The twinge of guilt nagging at her stomach on the drive back had eased away with that logical conclusion.

Olivia arranged her suit on a wooden hanger and hung it outside her closet door.

This was her day off. For years she'd worked seven days a week, squeezing in a little time each day for her children. But they had grown so fast, and she'd realized that she spent too little time with them. At that point she'd carved out at least one day exclusively for them.

Now that both of them were in college, Rochelle at Morehouse and Craig at Fisk, there was no reason to keep that extra day. But for some obscure reason, she had no desire to go to the spa today.

The empty nest syndrome crushed her, and settling into a routine without her children was difficult. She wasn't a clinging mother. She'd urged her children toward independence, and encouraged them to seek their educations at the schools that appealed to them. But she missed them more than she'd ever realized she would.

The quietness of the house only increased her loneliness. It was only two weeks ago that Olivia had rented a minivan and driven her daughter to Atlanta. Craig had his own car this year. She'd worried about him driving all the way to Tennessee, but a friend made the trip with him. And he'd had the cell phone she'd bought him, though he balked at taking it. She wouldn't hear of him driving that distance without an easy means of making a call.

In a sense, Olivia was glad the children were away, far away from her troubles. Children. Olivia chuckled. At twenty and eighteen, they were hardly children any longer.

It was hard thinking of them otherwise, though. It seemed like only yesterday that they were babies, and her most fervent worries were childcare, earaches and keeping a roof over their heads.

She sank to the edge of the bed and pulled on denim shorts and a white shirt. "Ah, Joe," she said. "I just wish you were here to see them grow. They are such lovely—*lovely*—people. And I'm not prejudiced." She reached for her cap on the bedside table.

Twelve years had passed since her husband's death, and not a day went by when she didn't have some small memory of him. Her son was the spitting image of his handsome dad, but his temperament was more like her father's. Her daughter had Joe's optimism and the ability to see beyond what the eye could see, just as her husband had when they'd decided to purchase their first home.

She hoped Clifton would find the person responsible for the robbery, for she felt strongly that someone was still out there enjoying the gains—someone who didn't care about how many lives he'd destroyed in the process.

Olivia left her bedroom and headed downstairs. It was obvious she was going to have to help with this case. She wasn't going to wait around idly while her twenty thousand dollars slipped into Clifton Zayne's fingers. She still had flutters in her chest from the blackmail payoff, and now this. Ten thousand was already gone.

Chapter 3

Clifton arrived at the office early the next morning, but he still wasn't the first one in. Bill Sawyer, his partner who had opened the firm two years ago, had already started the coffee and was sipping on a steaming cup. His jacket discarded, he'd rolled up the sleeves of a blue-and-white striped Perry Ellis shirt. Bill was "designer wear," while Clifton wore department store sale rack.

Bill and Olivia would make a perfect match, he thought, as both were elegant types. Clifton frowned. The image of Olivia paired with Bill didn't sit well with him. Then, too, Bill liked his women firm and stacked. He smiled. Olivia's teddy bear softness wouldn't appeal to his partner as she appealed to him. Perhaps once the case was over, he'd ask her for a date.

He wondered if she shared her life with someone special.

"You going to stare at that coffeepot all morning?" Bill stood in his doorway.

"Just thinking." Clifton snatched up a cup and poured, feeling foolish for letting a woman distract him. "How was the trip?" he asked to cover his lapse.

"Glad it's over. The family's fighting over who gets what. But at least we've found all of them." They'd been working on an estate case for the last few weeks, unearthing descendants of a ninety-year-old woman. Bill had flown to Alabama to try to identify a descendent.

"Was she the great-granddaughter?"

"She was."

Clifton sipped his piping hot coffee.

"How did things go with Mrs. Hammond?" Bill asked.

He shrugged his shoulder. "Do you remember the armored car gold heist that occurred twelve years ago?"

Bill relaxed stance was instantly alert. "Hell, yes. Who wouldn't?"

He explained her husband's connection and the blackmail attempt. "Did you know the detective in charge?"

"No." He shook his head. "But a friend of mine worked in that precinct, and he knew the detective. Let me call Ben and see what I can find out."

"Thanks, man."

Clifton made his way to his office, shrugging out of his brown and tan jacket, and hung it on the coatrack Veronica had brought from a yard sale. Taking his notebook from the breast pocket, he sat in his hand-me-down burgundy office chair. Setting his coffee on

a wooden coaster on the mahogany desk, he turned
on his computer and listened to the gyrations as it
booted up.

He clicked on the icon for the accounting program
they'd installed and opened an account for Olivia.
Scanning his notebook, he recorded the hours he'd
worked on her case so far, and details of his progress.
After exiting the program he heard Veronica enter
the outer office, calling out in a cheerful voice—
more buoyant than yesterday.

"Good morning, everyone," she called in a sing-
song fashion.

She almost floated past Clifton's door en route to
the coffeepot. She wore a red jacket paired with a
short, slim black skirt, and carefully applied makeup.
She hadn't painted her face yesterday, he thought.
It didn't take a detective license and twenty years of
police experience to deduce that she had an eye for
Bill. As far as he knew, Bill hadn't noticed her.

He guessed a woman might find his partner tall,
dark, and handsome, with an expensive tailored look.
Bill always had women pining for him. Clifton would
be darned if his sister would be one of them.

For a moment, he felt a twinge of protectiveness
for his younger sibling, but also recognized that at
thirty-five she wouldn't appreciate his interference.
Perhaps he'd have a man-to-man talk with Bill if he
did get around to noticing her.

Love was for fools. He had the occasional date, but
it didn't pay to get your heart tangled up with women.
The thought carried to Olivia. She was the soft, homey
type. When the case ended maybe he wouldn't try
for a date, after all. He wasn't a permanent kind of

guy, and she had permanence stamped all over her. Hadn't she stuck by a husband who'd been dead for more than twelve years?

"My day starts on a good note when the coffee is already made when I get in. Why do I always have to make it when you're out of town, Bill?" Veronica asked.

"Beats me," Bill said, laughing. "Maybe some of us suffer some deficiency."

"Oh, is that the reason?"

"Must be," he teased, walking out of the office to lean against the doorjamb.

Clifton ignored their reference to him. He loved good coffee, but his always came out strong enough to walk away. "Ronnie?" He called out as his sister passed his door again with her coffee.

"Yes?" She held the cup between both hands, a certain glow shining from her, a spring in her step. Perhaps Bill noticed, after all.

Clifton frowned. "Mrs. Hammond. Is she dating?" Veronica picked up on the gossip at the spa—women always gossiped. The passing of information in a spa was similar to that in a beauty parlor.

She shook her head. "No. Word is she's very private. She only goes out occasionally for business lunches or dinners. Why?"

"Just wondered if a suitor could be connected to her case."

"Oh. Her life's revolved around her kids, as far as I know. She's a nice lady. Kind to everyone. The blackmailer couldn't be someone associated with her."

"Even kind people have enemies, not always of

their own making," he said. The woman sounded like a saint.

He wondered if she'd had sex since her husband died. Twelve years without sex seemed extreme to him, especially since her husband died when she was young.

"You're looking nice this morning," he remembered to tell Ronnie.

"Oh, this old thing?"

"A lunch date?"

"Not likely." She rolled her eyes. Clifton smiled and shook his head as she left his office.

So Mrs. Hammond didn't date. Was that because she still pined for her husband, or had she centered her life around the spa and children, taking precious little time out for herself?

Sometimes Clifton wished he still believed in love and forever, as he had when he married nineteen years ago. Of course his wife's pregnancy had sped up their wedding, but he'd planned to marry her, anyway. Pregnancy wasn't the issue. He'd loved her, a love that had died years ago when she'd taken his son away from him.

Olivia marveled at how far she'd come. Twenty-six when Joe died, she'd been a naïve mother and wife, her sole concentration on her two children and her husband. Even though she knew she'd work outside the home one day and had taken college courses at the University of Maryland, she'd envisioned that work as being years down the road. And she'd thought she would teach.

After Joe's death, she'd taken more and more business and accounting classes. While cleaning homes for the very well-to-do in the Potomac and McLean area, she'd overheard conversations of weekend trips to West Virginia for spa treatment, and how the woman longed for day treatment closer to home.

At that point Olivia considered owning a spa of her own, and the seed of a business took root. She'd always viewed the cleaning business as a means to an end.

Late into the night after she put her children to bed and completed her homework, Olivia had researched the spa business. She added classes to her course schedule in preparation for the next step in her journey.

Now a sense of pride and accomplishment swept through her as she walked the well-kept halls of The Total Woman. She glimpsed a piece of dark lint on the eggshell carpeting and stooped, picked it up, and discarded it in the trash can in her French-decorated office.

A cream-colored French desk was one of the highlights of the well-appointed room containing matching credenzas and soft, cream leather chairs.

The decor was light and airy, designed to lift the spirits.

Women were ill-appreciated in this day of a power-hungry, go-for-the-jugular atmosphere. Women gave to everyone. Husbands. Demanding children who listened only when they wanted to, and were real terrors when the mood struck them. Demanding bosses. Even the dogs and cats at home. Who took the time to pamper women these days? Husbands were so caught up in their own careers that as long as clean shirts hung in the closet and freshly laundered underwear lay folded in layers in the drawers, they barely noticed women at all, except for the occasional rustle beneath the covers late into the nights when the house settled.

The Total Woman pampered. No complaints, no demands, just hours of pure, unabashed luxurious facials, body wraps, herbal treatments, pedicures, manicures, herbal cream massages to the sounds of soothing jazz and classical music. It even provided day care on a separate floor, well out of hearing distance. There was no impediment to enjoying The Total Woman.

Keeping manicurists and receptionists was another matter. Several employees had been with the company since its inception, and Olivia rewarded them with excellent benefits, including retirement and profit sharing. But others she hired stayed no longer than a few months to a year, and then moved on. She needed a few more dependable employees who were willing to make a career with The Total Woman. The tips alone put her employees above the average wage earner, and she paid a decent wage. Three years ago, she'd extended health care benefits that would rival those of many corporations.

The week before Chandra quit, Barbara, a manicurist, quit, and another had left four months ago.

Chandra, her receptionist of six months, had just quit with only a week's notice. Olivia thought that Chandra really enjoyed working there. The sudden departure puzzled her, because the young woman had shown an interest in facials. They'd discussed training, had actually been at the point of signing her up for courses.

Olivia slid her purse into her bottom drawer and opened the blinds to the window overlooking a small park. A few flowers still bloomed, though the leaves had started to turn yellow. Soon they'd be orange and rust. Fall displayed a lovely palette of colors.

Janice Kaiser entered the office adjacent to Olivia's. The women greeted each other, and Olivia went to Janice's door to talk about their personnel problems.

"Janice, I think we should consider part-timers for the receptionist position. Working mothers who want additional income but also crave more time with their families may work out better."

Janice glanced up from her computer screen and peered at Olivia from the top of her half-glasses. "We have several part-time applications. I'll set up the interviews."

"Thanks, Jan." Janice had been at the spa for five years, now. She knew every facet of the business, and the two women had both filled in when they were short of employees.

"How is Jackie's daughter working out?" Olivia asked.

"Very well. Judy learns quickly. It hasn't taken her long to grasp our techniques."

Olivia sighed. "I just hope she lasts."

"She's almost through with training. She wants a full-time position starting next month."

"Talk to her and see if some of the graduates from her class might be interested in a position. Now that some of the physical therapy programs are sending more and more of their patients here, we need more masseuses." Judy had worked for her part-time since high school, and had always been dependable. Since she'd been with them so long, the spa paid for her training.

"Debra was looking for you. Said she'll stop by your house tonight."

Olivia nodded, then remembered Janice was closing that night. She wasn't due in for a couple of hours yet. "What are you doing here so early?"

"I had some paperwork to finish before the late crowd."

Olivia cleared her throat. "Do you remember that vacation I've been talking about?"

"Uh-huh."

"I'll be taking more time off for the next two to three weeks at least, maybe longer. Not every day, but I won't be in on a regular basis. Do you think you can handle things without me?"

Janice rubbernecked, then she chuckled. "The iron woman's taking a vacation?" Suddenly she frowned, and her hand gripped the edge of her desk, pushing herself up. "Something's wrong. What is it? Is it the kids?"

"No. No." Olivia held up a hand. "Nothing's wrong. I just want a little time off, that's all."

"Are you going away?" She looked questioningly at Olivia, dropping back into her seat.

"I'm not sure yet."

"Are you okay?" A frown still marred her features.

Olivia groaned. "Can't I take a little vacation?"

"Sure, sure." The frown hadn't left when Olivia ambled to her office. Olivia shook her head. Hadn't she taken any time off in the last seven years? Thinking on it, she supposed she hadn't. Well then, it was about time she did—although this vacation had a purpose. It would allow her time to help Clifton investigate this robbery and determine who was blackmailing her.

She wondered what progress Clifton had made so far, and stifled the urge to call him.

Instead, she considered indulging in a body wrap just before seeing him again. One could sweat off ten pounds that way. But the other twenty would still be with her. *Scratch that,* Olivia thought, chastising herself—yet again—for her lack of willpower. She'd splurged on an omelet and pancakes this morning.

Why did she do that to herself? Afterward, she always regretted the impulse—always after, never before. With her, it was always *I'll start tomorrow. Today I'll splurge to prepare myself for doing without.*

The phone rang, and Olivia's hand went to the receiver and held it to her ear. "Good morning," she said in a soft, uplifting professional voice. "Thank you for calling The Total Woman. How may I help you?"

"Clifton Zayne here."

"Yes, Mr. Zayne?"

"I need the names and addresses of your employees, including those who are no longer with you, and your friends."

"I fail to see why that's necessary. My employees wouldn't"—Olivia noticed Janice passing her office and lowered her voice—"do something like that. They're like family."

"You'd be surprised what family can do. Many times in cases of this nature, it's the person you least expect. Could even be a trusted friend."

"Could you hold a moment, please?" Pushing from

her desk, Olivia hiked to her door, and closed it. Returning to the other side of her desk, she snatched the receiver and punched the blinking button. She leaned against the wooden edge angrily.

"Mr. Zayne."

"Yes?"

"Being a detective is one thing, but paranoia is entirely another issue. At seventy dollars an hour . . ." She gritted her teeth. "I expect you to focus on the heist, and the blackmailer."

"Mrs. Hammond. I'm doing my best to make sure you get seventy dollars an hour worth of services out of me. Please get me the list."

Olivia tapped her foot against the carpet, letting the silence stretch. "I'll see what I can do," she said finally.

"Thank you, Mrs. Hammond."

Olivia dropped the phone on the cradle and rounded her desk, sinking into her desk chair. She left the door closed, in case someone passed and wondered why she was so angry. What had the man been doing so far, if the best he could do was to request a list of her employees and friends? Her closest friend was Debra. She'd trust her life in Debra's hands. More—and this was saying a lot—she'd trust her children's lives with Debra. To have Clifton snoop on her best friend would be the worst kind of insult.

What kind of life had this man led that resulted in such sweeping distrust? She realized that a little healthy suspicion was essential for an effective detective. But snooping into her friends' and employees' business was taking cynicism to the extreme when the case didn't revolve around them. Then, too, Olivia thought with a hint of cynicism, it was an excellent tactic for elevating his fee.

The only thing that kept Olivia from looking for another detective was the fact that Clifton had discovered the whereabouts of a kidnapped little girl when everyone else had given up hope. She'd read an article about it. He'd been tenacious and thorough. Perhaps this was what it took to solve a twenty-year-old case.

She would still keep an eye on him.

Clifton looked through everything Olivia had given him again: Photos. Articles. Names. Notes.

"The cop, Carl Nelson, retired five years ago. But," Bill said, strolling into Clifton's office with his hands in the pockets of trousers that didn't display even one wrinkle, "he's got Alzheimer's. Some of his knowledge is skewed. He sometimes confuses one case with another. I don't know how much help he'll be, but he's willing to talk to you about the heist. He lives with his daughter in Potomac Beach."

"It's a start."

Sliding his hand out of his pocket, Bill handed Clifton an index card with Nelson's name and address on it.

"Directions are on the back."

Clifton took the card, nodding his thanks, then Bill left for his own office. The digital watch on his wrist displayed 11:15. The drive shouldn't take more than an hour. He ignored the ringing phone and Veronica's modulated voice in the outer office as he tightened his tie and donned his .38 and sports jacket.

He didn't go very far without his weapon. He sailed past her desk.

"For you, Cliff." She stopped him just as he reached the outer door.

He sighed, reached across her desk and took the phone from her, depressing the lit button.

"Clifton Zayne here."

"Mr. Zayne. This is Olivia Hammond. I'll get the list you requested to you tomorrow morning. In the meantime, I wonder if you've made any progress so far."

They'd met less than twenty-four hours ago, and she expected a progress report already? "I've followed some leads, and I'm on my way to interview the officer who was in charge of the case."

"Oh. Good."

"I'll be sending you weekly reports."

"Well, I should hope so."

"It's company policy."

"I see. Well, I'll let you get to that interview, then." Her tone was brusque and businesslike.

She disconnected, and Clifton slowly deposited the phone on the cradle, shaking his head and looking at it thoughtfully. What the hell was it about that woman that kicked his heart into overdrive when he was near her or talked to her?

"Do I see a smidgen of interest on your face?"

Clifton straightened and glared at his little sister. "You must be kidding."

"It's the same look you had as a teenager when one of your girlfriends called you or you were trying to hit on someone."

"I left puberty more than twenty years ago, lady."

"Doesn't matter. You still look at the phone forever after you hang it up when you're interested. I know."

Clifton didn't like the idea of his sister reading him so easily. "You'd better think about your own love life."

"Big brother, I can take care of mine *and* yours. And it's about time. If you need pointers, I'll be happy to lend you one of my romance novels."

Clifton ignored her and left, slamming the door behind him. He was sure he heard her laughter on his way down the corridor.

Once Clifton left the traffic behind on Route 50, he lowered the windows to let the breeze slap across his skin. It felt darn good. He stopped for gas at a discount station and engaged the lever so that the gas would pump by itself. Opening the car door, he retrieved his cell phone. Leaning against the door, he dialed his son's number.

Allen picked up after the first ring.

The greeting was stilted, but they waded their way through. "Do you think you can spend the weekend with your aunt and me?" Clifton asked.

"I don't know. I just got here."

"Your aunt and I would really love to see you. We'll fix your favorite food." In the silence that ensued, Clifton expected an immediate denial, and hated that he had to cajole his own son into a visit. They should have an easygoing kind of relationship by now in which they could just enjoy each other man-to-man, not this walking on eggs kind of conversation.

"All right. I'll see you Friday night."

"I'll e-mail you the directions."

They disconnected. Clifton had bought his son the car his junior year in high school, and he'd gotten him a new computer in July. His son was an engineering major, and Clifton hoped a computer in his room would make things easier for him. The teenager had complained that the computer Clifton had bought him three years ago was outdated.

Even though Clifton paid child support and bought his son the little extra things he'd always asked for, he realized that the most crucial element missing in Allen's life was his father's presence. That was why he'd moved to Maryland. He hoped that over the next four years they could carve out some kind of meaningful relationship.

The few weeks they spent together during the summer weren't enough. Even though the custody agreement was for the whole summer, his son usually had a job and activities that kept him with his mother. Attaining a peaceful relationship was always easier in theory than in actual life.

The lever clicked and gas stopped pumping. Clifton hung the nozzle up and went inside to buy a soda, then paid for his gas and drink. Soon he was on the road again, heading east.

He passed fields of peanuts yet to be harvested. Several roadside fruit and vegetable stands displayed pears, apples, tomatoes, cucumbers, cabbages, and more. If the stands were still open when he returned, he might stop and purchase some fruit.

His favorite dessert was apple pie, but he didn't have the knack for making them. His were usually

Sara Lee's from the frozen food department. He'd bet Olivia could bake a pie to make the mouth water.

In another hour he reached his destination—6215 Rosedale Court, located in a quiet neighborhood on a street of Cape Cod and ranch-style homes, each with well-maintained yards and fading flowers. Huge, well-developed trees attested to the age of the neighborhood.

The sun had disappeared behind the clouds as he parked across the street from the house near the end of a cul-de-sac. The weatherman had predicted rain. *Guess we'll be getting some,* he thought. He noticed an older gentleman working in a flower bed.

The white house held a fresh coat of paint, as did the green storm shutters.

He cut the engine and opened the door of his car, making sure he depressed the lock before closing it. Then he turned and crossed the street. He'd taken two steps when a young woman walked onto the front porch, carrying a laden tray.

"Dad," she called. "I fixed tall glasses of lemonade. Take a break with me?"

The man straightened slowly, but not completely. He swiped the back of his hand across his forehead and glanced toward the sky, easing himself bit by bit into a straight position. He'd turned a darker brown from sun exposure.

"I want to finish separating these irises before the rain comes."

"I'll help you later on this evening, but I need a break. Come on. I want to talk to you." Her round chestnut face split into a convincing smile.

"You're always wanting to talk about something.

Talk, talk, talk." He frowned at the woman Clifton presumed was his daughter, then looked at the gathering clouds.

"Don't be so fussy. Come and join me," the woman said patiently, unloading two, tall, flower-painted glasses and a pitcher of lemonade with lemons floating inside onto a small round table situated between two wicker chairs. This woman knew how to handle her father.

He grasped the bib of his cap and straightened it. "A man can't even tend his flowers in peace with you around." Slowly, he ambled to the house and up the steps, holding the railing for support.

Clifton walked up the bordered walk and greeted them when he reached the porch. "I'm Clifton Zayne," he said, and explained who he was.

"We've been expecting you, Mr. Zayne," the woman said, approaching him and extending a hand. Clifton noted the calluses on her palm when he clasped her hand in his. She wasn't afraid of work.

"Call me Clifton," he offered.

"Who're you?" the older man said.

"Dad, this is the investigator interested in the gold heist. You remember a call from Ben Williams, don't you? You always talked about that case."

"Damn investigators. Do nothing but get in the way." He frowned at Clifton and pulled off dirt-encrusted gloves, slapping them on the table. His daughter discreetly piled them on the floor next to his chair.

"Afternoon, Mr. Nelson." Clifton started up the steps as Nelson's daughter handed the man a damp towelette.

He grumbled as he wiped wrinkled hands that were darker than his arms and showed signs of arthritis.

"Have a seat, Clifton. I'm Marlene." She filled two tall glasses and offered him one.

Clifton nodded his thanks.

"You can talk while I go inside for another glass. Make yourself comfortable," she said to Clifton, and disappeared behind the screen door.

Clifton sat in the chair opposite Nelson, who took huge gulps of lemonade, eyeing Clifton cautiously. Clifton sipped his own drink, and wasn't disappointed with the homemade concoction. They sat silently, basking in their own thoughts.

They were silent so long that a blue jay flew to a bird feeder hanging from a low limb of an oak tree in the yard, taking up seeds in its beak. A soft wind gently rustled the leaves. It was a peaceful place to retire, Clifton thought. What a gentle way to live, worlds apart from the hustle and bustle of city life.

"Why are you interested in the heist?" the man finally asked.

"Do you remember Olivia Hammond?"

Nelson nodded.

"She's being blackmailed. The blackmailer said that they could prove that her husband was involved."

He nodded. "Had a hard time of it after her husband died. Younguns." He shook his head. "Don't think of the future. No insurance. A falling down house with nothing but mortgage payments and repair work. Had to rent out to two families to help her pay for it."

Clifton nodded and waited. He'd read between the lines that life had been tough after her Joe had died.

He rubbed the prickling sensation at the nape of his neck and chastised himself for being jealous of a dead man because of a woman he'd barely met—a client, at that. Joseph Hammond had some kind of power over Olivia. But then he realized that the couple should have cared for each other. Their marriage was as it should have been. It spoke volumes about the kind of woman she was, of the kind of man Joseph Hammond had been. Their closeness was far removed from the kind of marriage he'd had.

"I couldn't tell if he was part of the heist or not. But I know there was someone who planned it, and we didn't find him—or her. If he was part of it, he sure as hell didn't tell her where the gold was." Nelson stood slowly. "Be back in a minute. I put some things together for you."

He went into the house and returned three minutes later with a manila envelope and handed it to Clifton. "You can keep that." He eased himself into the chair and retrieved his glass.

"That was the most baffling damn case of my career. Always stuck in my craw that all that loot was never found. And somebody's out there laughing their guts out at us. Been laughing at us for twelve years, selling that gold on the black market."

"Why do you think her husband may have been involved?"

Nelson gazed at him for several long seconds. "Simon was supposed to meet me that night, said he had some information. He was killed on his way. I always thought that he ran scared at the last minute and was going to turn himself and the others in, and they got to him before he could talk to me."

"Simon? Simon who?" Clifton asked, a certain chill chasing down his spine.

"Simon Judd. You know. One of the Judd cousins in the bank robbery."

"What bank robbery?"

"The Judd brothers. The ones who held up the Twin National Bank. We cracked that case in four days," he said, clearly pleased with their performance.

Disappointment crowded Clifton.

"What about Joseph Hammond?"

Nelson put his glass on the small round table and closed his eyes. The sounds of nature surrounded them. "Who are you talking about?" he finally said.

"I don't think he's going to be any more help to you," Marlene said quietly.

The sound of her voice startled Clifton. He wondered how long she'd been standing there listening to them.

"Those cases have become very confusing to him." She walked to her father and put a hand on his shoulder.

Clifton regarded the man, who drank his lemonade. He captured a piece of ice and crunched on it and started humming a tune. What a shame. Bill had told Clifton of the many cases Nelson had solved. He was once thought the best detective in his division. Even in these enlightened times, modern medicine had a long way to go.

Clifton thanked Marlene and left a card in case Nelson remembered anything he could use.

He glanced at his watch. Since he was more than halfway to Chester Town, he headed east for an impromptu visit to Harvey Cooper. Rain finally came, a gentle sprinkling, just enough to wet the road and dampen the crops.

As the miles sped by the rain stopped, and brilliant sunshine replaced it. Clifton wondered if Joe had planned to meet Nelson that night, and if so, why? He wondered how much Olivia knew about it. Some nagging sense told him that Olivia knew more than she let on. He never forgot that clients always held something back—sometimes intentionally.

Chapter 4

Olivia had put off her exercise long enough. Without giving herself the opportunity to back out, the next morning she donned black spandex shorts that reached her knees and an oversize T-shirt hitting mid-thigh and started her warm-up stretches. By seven, she began her walk through the neighborhood.

She'd stopped her exercise routine the day she drove her daughter, Rochelle, to Atlanta. During the summer, Rochelle had walked with her three to four mornings each week. After the trip, even the thought of walking alone had her cleaning her son's bedroom rather than what she really should be doing. Lord, what a mess Craig had left. Packing at the last minute—as he always did—had left no time for straightening. While folding swim trunks and vacuuming, Olivia had really missed them, and had called both of them. She realized she couldn't call them every

time the mood hit her. But she'd needed to hear
their voices—anything to make them seem closer
somehow, and not hundreds of miles away.

They'd encouraged her to get a life of her own,
but they were her life. For the last twelve years her
life had revolved around her children and her work.
She definitely needed a change, but what?

Olivia stopped at a corner, looked for oncoming
traffic, and crossed the street.

When Rochelle walked with her, they'd talked
about her daughter's friends, her hopes, dreams, how
she felt about leaving home for the first time. Her
daughter's eyes had sparkled. The world was hers for
the taking, and Olivia felt lighthearted that she was
so exuberant and didn't feel hampered. She wanted
her children to explore and seek their desires. She
wanted them to live life to the fullest.

For her, life seemed the exact opposite. The journey seemed lonely with no one to share secrets with,
or laughter over something silly she encountered on
her jaunt. There was no fun in walking alone.

A motor revved just before it shot out of the garage.
Olivia stopped short and got her mind on her surroundings. Exercise could be hazardous, but never
boring, she thought as she proceeded. She greeted
a spandex-clad walker listening to a Walkman as she
jogged, passing Olivia while pushing a jogging
stroller. The baby's head, covered with a white cotton
cap, bobbed when the stroller hit a bump. *Now that's
the kind of dedication I need,* she thought as the duo
disappeared around a corner. Olivia resembled the
turtle, while the other woman was definitely the hare.

Arriving at her mile mark, Olivia swiveled and headed for home.

She had arranged an appointment with Sally Palmer for nine that morning. Sally was the wife of one of the guards, Lawrence Peters, who had died during surgery from a gunshot wound he'd suffered during the robbery. Olivia had dug through old Christmas cards to find her address. Sally had remarried three years ago, and Olivia had attended the small wedding.

After the walk she unearthed weights, dusted them off, and put herself through torturous stretches, sit-ups, and resistance exercises, all the while wondering if it was worth the excruciating effort. She definitely didn't have the proper attitude, she thought as she struggled through the last leg lift. Since she was already reclining, she rested where she was a few minutes before she gathered the energy to drag herself upstairs to the shower. Letting the hot water sluice over her body soothed her long-unused muscles. She made quick work of washing, and dried herself with a fluffy Egyptian cotton towel. Dressing in navy slacks and a knit shirt that reached mid-thigh, she marched downstairs to breakfast.

Standing in front of the open refrigerator door, she was tempted to eat a buttery, rich, blueberry muffin, along with eggs and sausage. Her hands had wrapped around the plastic-covered muffin, lifted it off the shelf. Olivia closed her eyes, thought of the walk and the tortuous exercises, and suddenly put it back. She settled for two slices of toast with nocalorie margarine spray topped with grape jelly, a banana, and a cup of yogurt for calcium.

She only hoped the fare was enough to keep her from snacking later on. Sitting at the table and looking at her food, she thought of how fit and trim Clifton was, and sucked in her stomach. Chocolates, muffins, pecan pies, always lifted her spirits for a few minutes, but only for a few.

Rochelle was worried because the doctor had finally put Olivia on blood pressure pills. He'd said if she lost the extra weight, she'd probably be able to go off them. She was the only parent her children had. She wanted to be around for them.

Oprah looked good on TV, Olivia thought. If Oprah could lose the weight, then so could she. She laughed— a hollow sound. How many times had she said that? She bit into the toast. At least with jelly, it was decent.

All the deliberation about food couldn't keep the thoughts of the blackmailer suppressed. The one percent fat peach yogurt went down smoothly. This was only Clifton's second day on the job, but she wondered again how much information he'd gathered. She'd faxed employee information to his office last night.

Olivia knocked on Sally's door precisely at nine. She and her new husband now lived in a lovely, single-family brick home in Fort Washington.

Sally was a nurse, and had been on duty in the emergency room the night of the robbery. She had always said she loved the activity of the emergency room. Her skills were always well honed, and she used them all. The pay had been added incentive.

"Are you still working the emergency room?" Olivia asked her, settling onto the olive-green couch.

She shook her head. "I haven't worked it in two years. I'm a surgical nurse now."

They sat in the family room, where a ten-by-fifteen framed wedding portrait of Sally and her new husband was centered on a round table covered with floral pattern skirting. Various portraits of the children were neatly arranged around it. Olivia focused on the portrait of the couple, then on Sally. She'd gotten on with her life. Sally looked very happy, and Olivia was glad she could put the past behind her, while the past wouldn't leave Olivia alone.

Sally was the same age as Olivia, and she wore black stretch pants with an oversize red shirt buttoned down the front. Her hair, worn in a French twist, exposed an unblemished dark face with obsidian eyes.

They talked about their children and caught up on the last three years before Olivia broached the subject that had brought her there.

"I want to talk to you about the robbery. You know all of our husbands were under suspicion after it happened."

Sally nodded. "That was such an awful, awful time."

"Do you remember anything special or unusual about that time? I know Joe was upset after the other men were killed." Lawrence, five years older than Joe, was senior and more experienced then the other men on the truck. He'd died during surgery.

Sally frowned. "You know, I was just thinking about the robbery the other night." She was silent for a moment, as if she were gathering her thoughts. "I talked to Lawrence a minute before they took him into surgery. He kept trying to tell Ray something. He seemed anxious. But you know how it was. I was so frightened, I couldn't be sure of anything. I just knew I was losing him. All the blood . . .'' She exhaled slowly—a long, long breath. Even after twelve years, the events still ripped her apart, as they did Olivia.

"Do you know what he meant by that?'' Olivia asked her quietly.

She tightened her mouth and shook her head. "I have no idea.''

Olivia had read over everything before she made copies for Clifton. "Do you mean Ray Wheeler?''

Sally nodded. "He made it to the emergency room just as they wheeled Lawr in. Lord, I remember just like it was yesterday. I asked him if he knew what Lawr had meant, and he didn't. He thought with all the pain, Lawr could have been saying anything, even talking out of his head. He probably didn't know what he was saying.''

"Umm.'' It didn't make any sense to Olivia, either, but she'd tell Clifton. Maybe he knew something, or eventually would. More than likely that was wishful thinking.

"Why this sudden interest? We haven't talked about this in years.''

"I just took the kids off to college, and I was thinking about Joe and the fact that they never solved the case.''

Sally reached out and squeezed Olivia's hand, then straightened. "You know it's time for you to get on with your life.''

"It's not easy to trust someone the way I did Joe,

you know? We grew up together—knew everything about each other. We really trusted.''

''I felt the same way at first. And then Paul came along.'' She smiled. ''He treated me like spun gold. It made me feel so special again.'' She glanced at the portraits on the table. ''And he loved my children, too. It's not every man who's willing to take on another man's children.''

A giant lump lodged in Olivia's throat. ''I'm happy for you.''

Sally smiled. ''You need to put this robbery behind you so you can make room for someone special to come into *your* life. It happens sometimes when you least expect it. It did for me. I certainly wasn't expecting Paul.''

''This robbery has always left me feeling like something's not quite finished, you know?'' Actually she did feel that way, with Joe's dying in the hit-and-run so close after. Olivia stood. ''Well, I won't keep you.''

Sally walked her to the door. ''Stop by any time. Don't be a stranger.''

''I won't.'' Olivia left, thinking that perhaps after she lost more weight, men might take interest in her again. She wasn't a spring chicken anymore. Older men all seemed to seek younger women. Still, Olivia needed more in her life. And the only way she'd get someone like Clifton to give her a second glance was to shed thirty more pounds.

She was being silly. She couldn't lose weight in the hopes of attracting a man. What would she do if she lost the weight and he wasn't interested? Gain it back?

Absolutely not. She couldn't lose weight for a man. She couldn't do it for people with better metabolisms, who looked down their noses with superior attitudes as if the weight said it all. When people were overweight, it was there for all to see. Often, others didn't take the time to learn the good qualities—like warm, caring dispositions.

If she lost more weight, she'd do it for herself. Because she wanted to feel better. Little steps like the walks each morning would keep her focused.

She'd been restless for the last month. Her first inclination was to fill her schedule with work, but perhaps the time had come to step back and contemplate. She had never taken time for herself in all these years. Always, there were things that needed to be done, and only Olivia could do them.

Clifton started his workday typing up notes from yesterday. He would have preferred completing that chore last night, but his trip to Chester Town had left him returning to the city late, and he drove directly home.

Cooper had been out of town on business, due to return a few days before taking off for Spednic Lake in Maine on a fishing trip.

Clifton had driven to his house. His wife had answered the door. Although the house was definitely upper middle class, it was within the means of a two-income family—especially when the wife was principal of a local high school, and the husband the branch manager of a bank.

Veronica had printed out information about Cooper from the database. He and his wife weren't big spenders. Though they paid many items by credit cards, they weren't extravagant, and paid the balances off by the end of each month.

Still, he'd been a high-ranking employee at Town Security, and Clifton would interview him, as he would the others.

Clifton opened the package Nelson had given him. It contained Xeroxed copies of photos of the crime scene, forensic details, the location of the heist— everything that Nelson had probably gathered before the FBI took over the case. Nelson had probably been angry when they'd walked in and excluded him. Real animosity flowed between the different government agencies, and even more between police officers and PIs. He guessed Nelson realized that he wouldn't be completing the investigation during his retirement as he'd planned, and had opted to pass the information on.

This was just the kind of case a retired officer would sink his teeth into and thrive on. Nothing taxing on the schedule. Time to think and research. Spending just a few hours each week interviewing, leaving enough time for fishing, gardening, or some other hobby. That could even save a marriage, not being under the wife's feet all hours of the day, getting on her nerves.

Clifton lamented. Alzheimer's. What a waste.

Clifton kept coming back to Joe, and Nelson's last skewed statements. Was Joe going to meet Nelson, and did Olivia know about it? He turned that over in his mind while he looked in his notepad for his next step—an interview with Sally Palmer. Information on her had emerged when he'd taken a trip to the court-house and sifted through the archives.

Clifton could save time and talk to these people over the phone, but the interview process was more than gathering data. Personal contact was necessary. A PI was a human lie detector. He needed to interpret the person's body language, to determine if they were telling the truth or if they knew more than they let on. A detective couldn't see a twitch of an eye over the phone, or aggravated hand gestures.

He arrived at Mrs. Palmer's house at ten and discovered that Olivia had just left. Mrs. Palmer was very suspicious, because he had come on the heels of Olivia's visit.

Instead of going to his next interview, Clifton drove straight to Olivia's house.

She lived in a subdivision of large homes and up-scale two-garage townhouses. He parked in front of her garage, taking his time to scan the neighborhood. He noticed movement of the curtains in a house directly across the street from Olivia. When Clifton used his peripheral vision to look from the side, he realized a man was sitting there, peeping out of the window. He filed the information in his memory.

Clifton glanced in both directions. For the most part, the neighborhood seemed quiet. He assumed most of her neighbors worked during the day.

All the townhouses had bricked fronts, most with two-car garages and little glass windows. The shrubbery was so large that the townhouses had to at least be five years old. Small flowers still struggled for survival before the fall frost.

He walked the short distance to the door and rang the bell.

It seemed like only a moment before Olivia

answered it, her cheeks vibrant from rushing, her eyes alive and sparkling. She wore navy slacks with a white vertical striped V-neck top. The outfit had a slimming effect. He regretted that she hadn't worn a skirt, giving him a glimpse of her legs; but the V-neck displayed the upper curves of her breasts. The view wasn't a total loss, after all.

Something long dormant had awakened the moment he'd seen her in that floppy hat and sun-shades. Whatever it was never left, but grew stronger as the days wore on. *Dangerously stronger,* Clifton thought, *for a beginning PI.*

"Come in," she said, stepping back to let him pass. She closed the door behind him and motioned him to the living room, which was situated on the left. "I was drinking tea. May I get you a cup? Or I can brew coffee if you like."

"Tea will be fine," he said, glimpsing the bare hint of crimson lipstick on her lips. Most of it had worn off, leaving just a touch of color intact—just enough to highlight her face. He'd always thought lipstick did a lot for a woman's appearance. He imagined the pleasure of sucking it off her.

"Make yourself comfortable." She turned and pro-ceeded down a short corridor.

The formal living room was painted off-white with a patterned border along the top. A rose couch flanked by off-white-and-rose striped Queen Anne chairs lent an aura of warmth. Beautiful paintings added life to the walls. He wasn't disappointed.

In lieu of lingering where he was, he followed her. The white ceramic tile and light oak floors with beige cabinets opened up the kitchen so that it appeared larger than it was. The kitchen was neat but homey, with little knickknacks on the wall and countertop. On the table sat a bowl of fresh fruit. He leaned against the doorjamb and watched her as she poured tea from a floral teapot with a white background into her best china cups.

"Would you like sugar or cream?" she called out.

"One spoon of sugar will do."

She yelped and jumped a foot at hearing his voice close by. She spun, her hand clutched to her chest. "I thought you were in the other room."

"We can talk in here. I'll be more comfortable."

Questioning, she raised an eyebrow, spooned the sugar into the cup, and stirred. Setting his cup and saucer on the table at the end closest to him, she motioned him to a seat. Her tea was already there beside a notebook, the cup half-filled. He noticed a sheet of paper propped in the napkin holder, listing the foods she'd eaten for breakfast that morning along with the exercise. At the top, the day's date was written in a lavish scrawl. A Giant Food's chart nearby, pinned to a corkboard, displayed BMI information.

She topped her tea and dumped in a package of Nutrasweet and joined him at the table. She immediately realized the diet info was in plain view and snatched the papers out of the holder, jamming them under her notebook.

"So what have you discovered so far?" she asked, excitement creeping into her voice.

He leaned back. "A better question would be what have you discovered?"

That was all the opening Olivia needed. Taking a proactive step in interviewing, she'd been gratified that she actually had information to contribute. "Funny you should ask, because I talked to Sally Palmer today." She explained who Sally and Lawrence were.

Clifton stirred the tea. "Uh-huh."

"It seems he was trying to tell Ray Wheeler something before he died. Now that I've thought about it, do you think he could have thought Ray was the one responsible? Maybe you can concentrate your search on Ray. We don't know what it meant, but it's better than what we have." An unusual excitement took hold of Olivia and wouldn't let go. Taking her cup in her hand, she sipped her tea. She put her enthusiasm in the interview and not her fascination with Clifton.

"I've recorded it along with other information. That's exactly what Mrs. Palmer told me."

The cup chimed as Olivia set it on the saucer. Her balloon deflated. "You talked to her?"

"You're paying me to interview leads."

"Yes, well—"

"And I respect the fact that you're paying me, but do you realize you can compromise this case by saying the wrong thing to the wrong person? And the blackmailer is still out there. We don't know who it is. You could mistakenly run into him or her."

Olivia leaned back in her chair. "Well, it's not Sally."

"We don't know that. What if you stumble onto the blackmailer in your interviews? You'll put yourself in danger—grave danger. You don't know the kind of person you're dealing with here. Or whether it's one or many."

"It doesn't cost me seventy bucks an hour to talk to people. I thought I could help out."

"In the long run, it could cost you more than your money." Clifton sighed. "I'm a trained investigator. Can you tell if a client is lying or holding something back?"

"Maybe." Olivia picked up her tea cup again and sipped.

"For instance, I can tell that you held something back when we met two days ago."

The cup clattered in the saucer. "I don't see how. I told you everything I know." She glanced down at her saucer and then regarded him wearily. "I knew the authorities were suspicious when they started asking all those questions."

He leaned forward, his forearms on the table. "Did your husband ever talk to you about the heist?"

She shook her head. "No. I knew it upset him, but . . ." Her eyes narrowed and she tilted her head. "What are you implying?"

"I'm just covering all the bases."

Olivia leaned toward him. "Do you think my husband was part of it?"

"You pay me to investigate the case and determine who initiated the heist. Therefore, I have to keep an open mind and investigate everyone. They may have pertinent information even if they weren't involved."

She stood. "You're suspicious of my most trusted friends, and now my husband. When I'm paying good money for you to work for me, I expect you to at least believe what I tell you." She paced to the sink, rinsed her cup.

"I have to ask the questions."

If he didn't believe in her from the beginning, then he was little use to her. "If you don't believe in my husband, then perhaps you aren't the detective I need working on my case." Olivia rubbed her temples. He'd brought it all home. The fire that started in her gut exploded. All the old suppressed anger descended on Clifton Zayne. She'd had enough suspicion from friends, from police, from everyone. She'd had suspicion up to her neck. She'd be damned if she'd pay twenty thousand dollars for more of the same. She faced him, her lips tight.

Clifton ran a hand along his collar. "You can't ask me to investigate a heist and close down the lines of inquiry."

"Thank you for your services, but I'll find someone else." She started for the door and left him no option but to follow.

Clifton looked at his tea and sighed. His cup was almost full. The brew with the steam wafting to his nose tantalized him. He picked up his cup and gulped two quick sips before he shook his head and placed it back on the delicate saucer. Earl Gray was his favorite blend when it was brewed properly. He eased out of the chair and followed her to the front door.

Her jaw clenched, her eyes wintry, she stood by the opening, tapping her toes against the wooden floor. She looked soft, capable, vulnerable all at once. Clifton wanted to protect her. He wanted to gather her in his arms and tell her all would be well. He wondered what she'd do if he kissed her, but didn't dare.

"Good-bye, Mr. Zayne," she said when he didn't move quickly enough.

"Mrs. Hammond." He passed her, the wind from

the door hitting him in the back. So much for his first big case in Prince Georges County.

He started back to his car, but an inner sense prompted him to glance across the street. Light reflected off the binoculars pressed against the window. Clifton was willing to bet that nothing happened on this street that that man didn't know about.

He sighed regretfully at his own loss. Damn. He'd been on the case for two days, and he was fired. He'd *never* been fired from a job.

Memories came of cases snatched from him because he got too close to the truth—a mayor's relative, a commissioner's rich friend's son. Whether he worked for the public or as a hired investigator, there was always someone to answer to—always someone who could fire him when the going got tough.

When he got behind the wheel and started the motor, the digital clock displayed eleven forty-five—lunchtime. He started down the road and saw a McDonald's. He and McDonald's were good friends. He pulled into the drive-in window and ordered a burger and fries with a milkshake.

Driving away, he wondered about the next investigator Olivia would meet, wearing her oversized sunshades and big floppy hat. He wondered if she'd enthrall the next one as much as she'd enchanted him. He frowned, regretting that it wouldn't be his case. He realized that the idea of Olivia going to some other man bothered him on a personal level, and it shouldn't. This was a job, after all. He never mixed business with pleasure. But then, he'd never met Olivia before.

Her reaction was extreme for a woman who wanted

him to dig up the truth about the heist. As he merged with the traffic on the beltway, he wondered, again, what secrets she held from him.

Someone leaned on the doorbell, then pounded on the door. The rattling sounded as if they were about to break the door down. Olivia dropped the sponge in the bathroom sink and flew downstairs, wondering whether she should call 911.

"Olivia?"

She relaxed. It was only Debra Mann, but something must be wrong. She rushed to the door, opening it, and her friend rushed in.

"Are you sick?" Debra put a hand to Olivia's forehead.

"No." Olivia shook her head.

"Is it the kids? Are you on your way to them? Which one is it?" Her copper skin was flushed from rushing, and the angst which showed on her face alarmed Olivia.

"What are you talking about?"

"Janice said you were taking some time off."

Olivia relaxed. "A vacation. There's no emergency. Come on in out of the doorway."

Debra didn't budge. "You're taking a few days off work, just so?"

Olivia sighed, exasperated. First Janice, and now Debra, giving her questioning looks just because she took a little time from work. "What's wrong with that?"

"You don't take vacations. That's what. At least, unless you're taking the kids someplace." She headed for the kitchen, her hand clutched to her chest. "I need a seat. Janice scared me to death. Then I tried to call you, and you didn't answer the phone."

Instead of taking a seat, Debra took a glass from the cabinet and got water from the automatic water dispenser in the fridge. Then she plunked down into the same chair Clifton had vacated only an hour ago.

"What were you doing?"

"Washing the bathroom sink." Olivia went to the bathroom located next to the den and washed her hands. "Have you had lunch yet?"

"I went by your office to see if you wanted to lunch with me. That's when Janice told me."

"I'll fix something for us." She'd put together a tuna salad last night.

Olivia put two huge leaves of lettuce topped with a thick slice of a red juicy tomato on each plate and topped them with tuna salad. She lined a basket with foil and poured crackers into it, setting the basket in the middle of the table. She sliced Granny Smith apples, oranges, and cantaloupes, and added grapes, arranging it all on the plate to complement the salad. *Very simple,* she thought, *and very healthy.*

"We're eating light today," Debra said, refilling her water.

"We're trying, anyway."

"Looks good." Debra sat and forked up tuna. Then she bit into a cracker and groaned. "Girl, I just love your tuna."

Olivia smiled. As thin as a rail, Debra loved anything Olivia fixed, and ate enough to feed an army—didn't know the meaning of exercise. Where did it all go?

"I've known you since we were kids. Something's

going on," Debra said. "I don't care what you said. You don't just take a vacation for no reason. Not that it's a bad thing, mind you. I think it's a wonderful idea."

Olivia and Debra had been close friends since they were kids, and she didn't like keeping secrets. If Debra were in this situation, she'd want her to share it with her. Not that she could do anything, but that's what friendships were about.

"Well—" Olivia started.

"I knew it."

"About a week before I took Rochelle to school, I got this blackmail letter in the mail."

"What? Your life is cleaner and more boring than anyone I know. What do they have to blackmail you about?"

"The letter said that they could prove that Joe had something to do with the heist."

"That's garbage." Debra had known Joe for as long as she'd known Olivia.

"I know it is, but I paid the money, anyway."

"How could you do something so silly? Now, you've got them thinking they can come to you anytime they feel like it. What did the police say?"

"I didn't tell them."

Debra put down her fork and regarded her friend. "Are you crazy?"

"But I hired a private detective."

"That's better than nothing, I guess. But you should have called the police."

"And let them think that Joe had something to do with it? They didn't find anything twelve years ago. Why should I feel anything is different now?"

"You've got a point there."

"Then tongues will be wagging about Joe all over again. I don't want that. For Joe or the children."

"What does this detective think?"

"His first advice was to go to the police. But when I explained the situation, he took on the case."

"Wonderful." She nodded. "Is he any good?"

"He's Veronica's brother. You met her at the spa."

Debra frowned. "She works in the office with them, doesn't she?"

"Yes, and he's the one who found that kidnapped child a year ago when they'd almost given up hope."

"At least he's good." Debra forked tuna on another cracker.

Olivia speared a cantaloupe cube and held it in the air. "I fired him."

The fork clattered to the plate. "What for?"

"I don't think he believes my Joe is innocent. Asking me all these questions. Asking me if I told him everything. Snooping into my friends' business, and my employees. He got angry because I started doing a little interviewing on my own, like it wasn't my right."

"What *were* you doing interviewing?"

"Because he's costing me a darn fortune, that's why. Thought I could cut down on some of the work."

"You've always got to be sticking your nose into everything. Let the man do his job. Hire him back."

"I will not. He's suspicious of everybody, even you. If I'm paying him good money, he at least has to believe what I tell him."

"You're paying him to find the blackmailer. I know Joe is innocent. You know Joe's innocent. But we aren't investigators. We don't know how it works. And quite frankly, I don't care if he snoops in my life. I've got nothing to hide."

Olivia just looked mutinous.

"Get that stubborn look off your face." She reached across and patted Olivia on the hand. "Hire him back."

"I will not."

"What are you going to do when the blackmailers come back? Tell me that."

"I'm looking for someone else."

"You don't know anyone else. You were lucky to find him. Don't be stubborn about this, Olivia."

"I'll think about it."

Debra shrugged her shoulders, eyeing Olivia shyly. "You're interested," she said.

Olivia straightened in her seat, and lifted her chin. "I most certainly am not."

"Well." Debra leaned back into her chair, a grin splitting her face. "It's about time."

Olivia sighed. "He's built all nice and firm, like a male Adonis."

"You don't have to tell me. I was there when he picked up Veronica one day."

"You know how vain good-looking men can be."

"Give the man a chance, will you? He may not be that way. You don't know."

Olivia waved a hand. "I have too much to deal with to even be thinking of a man right now."

"When are you going to have time? When you're eighty?"

"We'll see."

"Just see that you rehire that man."

"I said I'll think about it."

They finished lunch. Olivia changed clothes and drove the short distance to the spa.

As soon as Debra left, Olivia had eaten the muffin she'd resisted earlier that morning. Then, in a fit of anger, she'd taken the rest and dumped them in the garbage. There was nothing else tempting to eat in the house. She promised herself she'd eat a light dinner to make up for her lapse. She'd started the day so well, too.

At one that afternoon Clifton returned to the office, his jacket slung over his shoulder. The heat had increased, and he needed a shower.

"Oh, there you are." Veronica held out a sheet of paper for him. "Ray Wheeler's divorce came through a year after the heist."

Clifton walked slowly to her desk and took the sheet of paper out of her hand.

"By the way, she just fired me."

"Already?"

"See what you can find on the other employees who knew anything about that cargo. And start on that list of employees and friends Olivia faxed."

"I though you were fired."

"I am. Her retainer will cover the cost."

"But . . ."

He entered his own office and read the sheet Veronica had handed him. "If she doesn't call me after she's slept on it, I'll give it up." Technically, the case was over, but he hoped she'd reconsider. Clifton had a strong hunch that Olivia hadn't heard the last from her blackmailer.

Chapter 5

"There's no sense in you pissing in your beer because you lost this case," Veronica said later that afternoon. "Come on, let's all go to The Palace." The Palace was a sports bar down the street from their office.

Veronica wore a fitted black pantsuit today, with pearls. "It's Happy Hour, and they're serving hot wings and celery sticks for no more than your McDonald's, Cliff."

"Sounds good to me." Bill joined them, donning his imported sports jacket. "I'm ready."

"Come on, Cliff. Don't be a spoilsport. You won't have to cook dinner."

A few minutes later, Clifton found himself at The Palace, munching on peanuts and pretzels while he waited for his basket of hot wings and celery. He realized that he didn't stand a chance for a date with

Olivia now. Then he smiled. When had he ever let a little discord dissuade him?

It was six, and the after-work crowd clamored in in droves. The seats at the huge, dark-stained bar were all taken, the bartenders working quickly and efficiently in the generous space behind it.

Posters of ballplayers—football, basketball, baseball—hung on the wood-paneled walls.

A group of businesswomen entered and began talking enthusiastically at a table next to theirs. One sister was a looker, and Clifton did a double take. Her eyes met his with steady intent. She was slim and tall, with breasts that were probably enhanced by more than nature, a complexion of smooth, rich, dark chocolate— exactly the kind of woman who usually appealed to him. She stood at least five-ten, and her skirt ended at mid-thigh, with legs that were more gorgeous than he'd seen in a long time. Slowly she crossed them. With his gaze, Clifton followed her practiced moves.

Had it been a month ago, he would have taken her up on her offer and even now would be strolling to her table, asking her for a dance, opening the game of pursuit—especially since the song playing now was Gerald LaVert, smooth, soft, mellow. He'd draw her into his arms and press her close to him with those long legs sliding back and forth against his thigh.

Her friends would have left tonight minus her.

Clifton gazed at the tall, chilled beer glass in his hand. He didn't want smooth and fake, he wanted real and soft. He wanted Olivia.

"Oh, great. The wings are here." Veronica dipped a wingette into the blue cheese dressing, closing her eyes when she tasted the treat.

Clifton took a long pull from his draft beer. The deterrent of a professional relationship with Olivia had ceased to exist. He'd give her a week and then he'd make his move.

By the next morning, Olivia had come to terms with her hasty decision. A night of tangling her sheets, tossing, turning, and debating had her bleary-eyed and irritable. At six she gave up the fight and threw back the comforter she'd fought through the night. Pulling on loose-fitting shorts and an oversize T-shirt, she went into the bathroom, brushed her teeth, and washed her face.

By the time she finished her warm-up stretches it was six-fifteen. She chastised herself for going off her diet—change of eating pattern—last night, yet again. The stress had been just the excuse she needed to stop at Giant's on the way home from the spa to purchase a pint of butter pecan ice cream.

At home, the empty nest syndrome had closed in on her. She missed her son and daughter more than ever. By 10:00 P.M. at least one of them would have been home. Craig would have come in and headed straight for the fridge for milk or soda, say a minimum of words, and sauntered down to the basement, where he'd moved that summer. He'd wanted his own space. Rochelle would have wandered in, kicking off her shoes, and sat at the table, ready to talk for hours about her friends or a date—or something.

Then Olivia had remembered she'd put a package of goobers in the freezer, thinking *out of sight, out of mind*. She'd eaten the pint of ice cream and the box of goobers last night before she settled down for a few minutes with an overwhelming sense of satisfaction. It took only fifteen minutes before the guilt stirred her conscience. As always, she'd felt guilty afterward. Too bad that guilt hadn't overridden the cravings *before* the deed was done. Olivia opened the door. Back at square one, *again.*

Closing the Velcro strand from which her house key dangled, she strolled down the sidewalk. More people were about at six than at seven, her usual time, she realized as she started her brisk pace. The morning was perfect for getting the blood pumping— not so cold yet that she needed a jacket, but not hot, either.

Then she thought of Clifton. She'd turned their conversation over and over in her head for hours last night. Was she being fair to him, or was she so upset at the idea of her husband being implicated that she'd reacted too hastily?

She had tried to be objective, tried to see the situation from his point of view, as Debra had advised. Her first thought assured her that Clifton was wasting time asking questions about her husband's state of mind about her friends. But he *would* have to search the backgrounds of everyone, including her Joe.

Her conscience nagged her again, pricking at the edge of her thoughts because Joe had been unable to sleep his last few nights. She'd expected his unrest. Who could sleep as soundly as a baby, without a worry, when they'd had guns trained on them—seen others die? She'd have been disturbed, too. Anyone would be. She couldn't expect any less from her husband.

In truth, part of her decision was based on the vibes

that sizzled between Clifton and her every time they were together, like a charge in the air, unseen but very much felt. Around Clifton she felt insecure, that she was being unfaithful to Joe's memory.

Olivia released a pent-up breath. Joe had been gone for twelve years now, and she was still very much alive. But mentally she still clung to Joe. It was time to let him go, to give herself time to live, to experience whatever joy life offered. It had been easy to neglect herself while she reared her children. But now they had their own lives. They didn't need Mom leading them every step of the way. She'd performed her duties and, like a bird, she had to let them fly on their own. She needed to live her life.

She had to deal with her reality, that the blackmailer would more than likely return as soon as the money ran out. Five thousand wouldn't last very long.

With anger taking over, as it always did when she thought of the blackmailer, she clenched her fingers around the key. She wasn't paying another cent of her money for something Joe didn't do. She'd worked too long and too hard for that.

Olivia stopped in unfamiliar territory. She'd passed her usual turning point. Pivoting, she retraced her steps. She was thoroughly warmed by now. The adrenaline from the anger and the walk energized her. But tension still rode her like a living thing.

It was just before seven when she opened her door—still too early to call Clifton. She showered and threw on a robe to eat her breakfast. This time she substituted oatmeal for dry cereal.

After brushing her teeth, she dressed in a gray suit and rose blouse, taking special care in preparing for her day. Back-to-back seminars meant she had to contact Clifton this morning or wait until late that afternoon. Olivia wasn't one to wait once she made a decision. Adding a gold necklace and matching earrings, she smoothed on a thin layer of foundation and applied a delicate shade of lipstick to match her blouse. Several brush strokes to her hair, and Olivia was armed for battle.

She dialed Clifton's office. Veronica answered the phone, informing her that he wasn't in. Olivia explained that she needed to talk to him that morning, that she'd be unavailable later on. Veronica gave Olivia his home number, saying she could probably catch him there. When she reached Clifton, he invited her over.

In an older, well-kept section of town, his address was very familiar to her. Debra lived only a block from him.

Olivia tore out of the garage, closing the door with the remote.

On the street where Clifton lived, a couple who appeared to be in their sixties speed-walked down the sidewalk. She passed ranch-style houses, two-storied and split-level dwellings. His house had huge, multipaned, curved windows that Olivia loved but didn't see in newer homes. As she slid out of her seat, a Pomeranian stood at a bay window next door, peering out. Its front paws on the glass, it began to bark incessantly at her.

Olivia pressed the doorbell, but no one answered. She assumed the car parked at the curb belonged to him. He must be around somewhere. He knew she would be stopping by. She pressed the button again, and waited. Seconds ticked by, but still no answer.

Riffling through her purse for pen and notepad, she jotted a short message and closed it in the screen door. When she heard someone approaching, she turned and almost fainted.

Clifton moved slowly toward her, his hands on his hips, his breath labored. Sweat trickled down his face, and his shirt was wet in patches. Wearing a muscle shirt and loose-fitting shorts which left little to the imagination, he looked so good that she lost her speech, and could only gape. Why couldn't she just look cool? She'd never been good at cool.

"Looking for me?" he asked, winded. He had gone running just after she called.

She didn't respond.

He smiled. "Hel—lo."

"I . . . yes." She nodded stupidly and cleared her throat. *Get a grip, Olivia.* She squared her shoulders and sucked in her breath, noticing that not an ounce of fat was visible on that hard body. His damp shirt stuck to his washboard abdomen, drawing her eyes— his muscles rippled every time he moved.

She coughed. "Yes, I have meetings all day, and wanted to see you this morning before I left."

He merely nodded and gazed at her as if he were waiting for something more.

"I'd like to rehire you. Perhaps I was a bit—hasty yesterday."

He stood at the bottom of the steps as they talked.

"As long as we agree that I investigate the case any way I see fit."

"You have to understand that my husband was an honorable man."

Clifton inhaled the scent of her delicate perfume with a breath that ended on a sigh. "Olivia, I'm not accusing your husband of anything. If he's innocent, nothing will show up in the investigation, will it? I'm just following leads." He wanted the right to reach out to her, to touch her, to stroke her smooth skin.

Her hand tightened around her purse strap. "Fine," she said. "But I still say it's a waste of time."

"Duly noted." He dropped his arms to his side to keep from touching her. "But, I'll repeat—being thorough is never a waste of time. It's little insignificant details that solve cases."

Olivia nodded, unconvinced. "Do I need to pay you more money?"

"Not yet." Goosebumps beaded on his arms as the sweat dried. Were the bumps from the contrasting temperature, or from Olivia's effect on him?

"Well." She glanced at her watch. "Thank you." She searched around for something else to say, and couldn't conjure a single thought. So she stuck out her hand.

He grasped it in his large, slightly callused one. His shake was firm, and he held on longer than was prudent. When he released her she moved toward her car, and he fell in step beside her. "I'll keep in touch," he said.

She smiled and inserted the key in the door. He opened the door for her. She looked at him, startled. "Thank you." She climbed in and settled in her seat.

He closed the door gently after her and backed away from the car, continuing to watch her as she backed out of the drive. It had been years since a man had performed the gentlemanly act of opening a door for her.

Settle down, girl, she said to herself. *Just shows that he was brought up with good manners.* But that small gesture had made her feel special.

Clifton strolled into the office on a jovial note. With an empty coffeepot in hand, Veronica glanced at him and shrieked when he picked her up and swung her around. "We're back in business," he said among her protests and laughter.

"Put me down, you big lug."

He set her on her feet. Bill wasn't in the office that day, so she wore plain slacks with a print top. Her appearance was professional, but the clothing wasn't designed to tempt. Bill was missing it all.

"Try not to blow it this time, will you?"

He regarded her. "I'll do my best. Hey, who's the PI around here, anyway?"

Ignoring him, she filled the pot with water, added the coffee, and turned on the machine. "Got some more information for you." She wandered to her chair.

"What is it?" he asked, sliding his hands in his pockets.

"I have employment information on all the names you gave me. It's on your desk."

"Ronnie?"

She glanced at him.

"How do you feel about Bill?"

"What are you trying to say?" She was instantly

defensive. Clifton knew he was on the right track. Might as well nip this in the bud.

"I'm asking if your feelings for him are more than professional."

"Cliff, you're broaching a topic that's none of your business."

"I don't—"

She stood, her hands on her hips. "Don't even go there. I'm thirty-five, and grown enough to deal with my life on my own terms—without your interference."

Clifton held up a hand. "I just want you to be careful with him. Bill isn't ready to settle down."

"Who are you to talk? You're the one who chased any hot mama in a skirt."

Clifton hadn't been that bad. Besides, he'd changed— Bill hadn't. "I'm just saying, be careful." With his parting shot, he sauntered to his office. Bill wasn't going to take advantage of *his* sister.

She'd stacked printouts in a pile in front of his chair. Clifton picked up the first sheet and read. The words blurred before him.

Hell, he couldn't control his own desire for Olivia. What right did he have to intrude in Ronnie's life? But that protective big brother role still clung, no matter how old she was.

That afternoon, Clifton drove by the scene of the heist. It had occurred in a wooded area off Tremor, situated about a mile from the beltway. He parked his car at the curb and slid out, gazing around. A great deal could happen in twelve years—new roads, new developments, new parks—but this area looked as if time had stood still.

He glanced at the sky as a plane descended, probably landing at Andrews, Bolling, or National Airport.

Clifton made for the grove of trees in back of him, listening to the sparse traffic, the noise from the planes and, although he was a mile from the beltway, its activity from transfer trucks and other vehicles made its presence known. Traffic never let up on the beltway. It was always there, steady, consistent, and noisy—just a little less at some times than others, but always present.

Clifton passed patches of trees and crossed two-lane, unmarked roads that wound through the park, past picnic tables, scattered grills, swings, and monkey bars.

He noticed an occasional car, saw squirrels scampering about, but didn't see another person. He plowed on. Finally he heard voices and, checking for landmarks, moved toward them.

Through another group of trees, he saw a development of townhouses that didn't look very old. He saw a "For Rent" sign in front of one and a "For Sale" sign on another. Not many people milled about today, but he noticed a 7-Eleven at the end of the street. He walked on.

At the 7-Eleven, he got a bottle of water and stood in line at the cash register. There was a steady flow of people buying gas, chili dogs, nachos—small items.

When his turn at the register arrived, he handed over the money for his drink. "Pretty warm out there today," Clifton said to the cashier, whose shirt was stained, his hair straight and short. He was from India, and looked to be about thirty.

"Yeah." He only had a slight accent.

"Do you know how long these townhouses have been here?"

"About fifteen years. I went to school in this neighborhood."

"Isn't this where that gold heist took place years ago?" Clifton asked.

"It is." He nodded. "Was the talk of the area for a long time." Clifton didn't detect anything unusual about his speech or reaction. Nothing indicated that he'd seen something during the heist. He would have been around eighteen.

Clifton thanked him and left. He'd return one evening when more people were about.

Olivia's last facial had been more than a month ago, when Rochelle performed the deed. After a stressful two days, she craved one. Making a beeline for the bank of phones after her last meeting, she called Janice, asking her to schedule one if space allowed.

An hour later, Olivia reclined in the room usually reserved for body wraps. Few customers requested wraps, and all the rooms designed for facials and massages were in use. If a customer required time after two, they needed to make an appointment two weeks in advance. Olivia had considered expanding, but decided not to just yet. An expansion would require more money, maybe even a new location. She liked where she was. And enough changes were

occurring in her life. She'd give it some thought next
year, perhaps.

All the specialists were busy with paying customers,
so she drew Janice. Janice and Olivia were both
licensed in the services the shop provided.

Leaving a hot towel on her face, Janice used circular
motions to massage Olivia's scalp in flowing, even
strokes. Olivia relaxed for the first time in days and
let her mind wander, determined not to think of the
blackmail.

She thought of Clifton and wondered how a thirty-
eight-year-old woman could approach a man who
interested her—who also worked *for* her?

Clifton interviewed two former Town Security
employees that afternoon. He came away with the
information that Ray Wheeler had been deep into
gambling when his wife left him mere months before
the robbery.

Wheeler was single and lived in an upscale townhouse off Beaver Street. Clifton parked in front of
his home and waited for Wheeler's BMW. He didn't
have long. After Wheeler parked, Clifton approached
him.

"Mr. Wheeler, I'm Clifton Zayne, a private investigator working with Reliable Insurance Company."
He handed him a card. "I'd like to talk to you about
the gold heist that occurred twelve years ago."

"Again? It's been years. We told them everything
we knew back then."

"They've been given additional information."

"What information?"

"I'm not at liberty to divulge it."

Wheeler swiped a hand across his face and glanced at his watch. "I can only spare a few minutes. You should have called first."

"I appreciate it. I understand you managed the division involved."

"That's common knowledge."

"I have reports that you were gambling heavily at that time."

"And that's your new information?" He tightened his lips in anger.

"As I said, I can't divulge my information."

Wheeler's gaze was direct and firm as he put his hands on his hips and leaned forward. "I paid off those debts with my share of the property after the divorce settlement, and joined Gamblers Anonymous. I didn't have to steal to pay it off. You probably already know that my wife left me because of the gambling. I'm straightened out now. The company knew about the gambling. I was told to get my act together, or else." He straightened. "I got my act together."

"Did you have any suspicions of other employees?"

"None. I don't believe it was an inside job. It couldn't have been."

"Why not?"

"We did thorough background checks of our employees, and additional checks every two years. There was nothing that indicated that anyone who knew the schedule was in dire straits."

"Except you."

He tensed, but continued as if Clifton hadn't spoken. "These people worked together, joked together, they knew each other's families. They couldn't have done that to a fellow employee."

"If you remember anything, please give me a call."

Clifton detected that Wheeler really believed what he said. But didn't the man realize that people really didn't know each other as well as they thought they did? The divorce rates, parents kidnapping their own children after unsatisfactory settlements, both attested to the fact that many people didn't know each other, after all.

Chapter 6

Clifton parked his black Taurus in front of The Total Woman at 6:00 P.M. Veronica's Camry was in the shop.

Reschedule her spa treatment? "Unthinkable," she'd said. Which left Clifton surrounded by a sea of women in the almost country-like complex.

Narrow walkways pinched between emerald green grass, vibrantly hued flowers and neatly trimmed hedges led the way to two-story buildings. Women hurried into the spa more than any of the other shops.

It must be rush hour.

Locking his door, he wondered what drew women to the place like bears to honey. He held the door for two of them to charge in ahead of him. One slowed just long enough to give him a long look and a sweet thank you.

Standing in line in the large room at the reception

desk, he listened to soft music which added just the right ambiance to the elegant tableau. Delicate womanly scents floated in the air. Facing front, he noticed that brilliant sunlight flashed through the glass wall, the other three walls papered in marbled off-white.

While the receptionist assisted customers at a glass-topped table, Clifton shoved his hands into his pockets and regarded his surroundings. Immense pastel prints on the walls lent a more open appearance. Plants along the bottom of the bank of windows immediately transported him to springtime freshness, yet the room carried just a hint of warmth.

Rows upon rows of neatly stacked bottles layered the shelves behind the receptionist, who also did double duty as cashier.

Clifton wasn't surprised that the place was every bit as classy as the owner.

Then he saw her, moving toward the door, engrossed in a conversation with a tall man who reached at least six-five. He wore a tailored, three-piece suit that was much more expensive than the suits Clifton wore. *A basketball jock in college,* Clifton postulated. He strained to hear their conversation, but their low modulated tones escaped him as they approached the door.

Clifton knew the instant she saw him. Her eyes widened, and he smiled at her startled gaze. His grin changed to a frown when the man said, "Let's do lunch next Wednesday and discuss it, Olivia." His pronunciation flowed like a caress.

Blinking, she tore her focus back toward the man. Her, "Why don't we?" didn't appeal to Clifton any better.

"I'll call you Monday," the man said with a practiced smile. Clifton gritted his teeth and swore.

The man encroached on his territory. Clifton could see Olivia now in one of those fitted suits. He wondered if she'd wear one of those big floppy hats with Mr. Slick. *He didn't think so.* And he considered how many lunches the man might squeeze in to work himself into a date.

Clifton knew right then and there that he couldn't wait any longer to move their professional relationship to a personal level. In another week, Mr. *Slick* would have talked her into a date well before the case was over, leaving Clifton in the cold.

When she looked elsewhere, Clifton set his teeth at the man's lingering looks and overly solicitous behavior. She was so busy debating with him that she didn't notice. And Clifton was well aware that a lively debate could heat a man's blood as quickly as a stroking hand. *Foreplay,* he thought.

"Hello?" she said tentatively, her eyebrows raised in question.

"I'm waiting for Veronica," he told her before she asked. "Her car's in the shop, and she asked me to pick her up."

"I'll let her know you're here," she offered.

"Don't bother." He dragged his left hand out of his pocket and glanced at his watch. "I may be a few minutes early. I'll be her enemy for life if I take her away before her time is up."

"It's good to hear that she enjoys her treatment here." The tense expression on her face eased. But Clifton wondered how he'd talk her into a date if she didn't want to be seen in public with him.

The very worst thing an investigator could do was to get involved romantically with a client. All the objectivity flew out the window at that point. Clifton had never had problems with disassociating work and pleasure before, but she'd been tantalizing him for days now with those prim suits and chic slacks. He wanted to peel them off piece by delicate piece to the softness beneath. Suddenly, he grew hot and wiped a hand across his brow.

"May I get you something to drink? We have all kinds of juices, coffee, tea."

"Juice." Clifton cleared his throat. "Thank you."

"Why don't you wait for her in my office?" She leaned toward the receptionist. "Susan, please buzz my office when Veronica Davis is through. Her brother will be waiting for her there."

The woman with the braids wrapped around her crown like a work of art, nodded.

Clifton followed Olivia through double off-white doors with brass knobs. He glimpsed the rhythmic sway of her hips as they continued along a wide well-lit corridor. Four offices with huge glass walls were on the right. The very last office was Olivia's. Passing through the secretary's office, absent the secretary, Clifton noticed a cooling cup of coffee on her desk and a sheet of paper she seemed to have been working on, carefully centered on the pink desk blotter.

Two doors led from there. He and Olivia entered the spacious interior of her office. She closed the door behind them, enveloping them into soft seclusion. The powder blue walls were a perfect complement to the off-white furniture.

Pulling juice out of a small fridge disguised as a

cabinet along the left wall, she motioned to a seat facing her desk, and Clifton sank into the soft, pale-blue-and-cream striped cushions.

Today two gold necklaces dangled at the V neck of her aquamarine pantsuit jacket. She took out a glass and poured the juice. Leaning over, she handed him the drink, giving him a glimpse of the top of her breasts.

Clifton checked the button on his jacket and shifted in his seat.

Skirting the desk, she settled in the office chair. "How is the case progressing?" she asked.

"We're doing a follow-up on everyone involved with the heist. Employees. Families of the robbers. Lots of legwork." He sipped his drink. Damn, it was hot in there.

She nodded, looking so confident and poised sitting behind her desk. He wondered again how to broach the subject of a date. Usually he had a ready line, but this time the answer mattered. The take it or leave it proposition of other dates were totally different. He felt eighteen again.

"Olivia," he started, inhaling sharply.

"Yes?" Her lyrical response gave him courage just as a discreet knock sounded on the door.

"Come in," she called out in a clear crisp voice.

Clifton stifled an annoyed glance as the door opened a crack, revealing Veronica carrying a gym bag. She glowed. Whatever the spa offered was definitely working.

"Hi," she said, stepping over the threshold. "I came to rescue you from my brother."

"All set to go?" Clifton stood, wishing she'd taken

five minutes longer. He'd deliver the weekly report to Olivia tomorrow morning—in person—and work in a date.

"Yes. And if we don't leave soon, I'll melt into the carpet, I'm so relaxed." Veronica paused, glancing from Olivia to him. "Olivia, we're having a barbecue at the house Saturday evening. Would you like to come?"

"Oh, I . . . I couldn't intrude on a family gathering." Her eyes met Cliff's briefly and skittered away.

"No imposition. Cliff's son will be there, and our other partner, who you haven't met. It'll be a fun gathering."

"Well—"

"If you hate to drive at night, I'll pick you up," Cliff said, silently thanking Veronica for her ingenuity. They hadn't planned any barbecue. His sister saw a bit too much at times. He'd forgive her.

"I don't mind—"

"I'll pick you up at five, then." No sense in giving her time to mull through it or call later with some excuse. She'd talk herself out of the dinner altogether.

"Will five work for you?"

"Yes . . ."

"Okay, we'll see you then." Clifton urged Veronica out of the office. He was a great deal more lighthearted leaving than he'd been when he arrived. Saturday would give him a chance to work his magic before Slick could put his stamp on her.

He opened the car door for Veronica.

She raised an eyebrow.

"Practicing rusty skills," he said. "Thanks, by the way."

"You're welcome," she said, and sank into the seat.

Clifton only wished that the dinner with Olivia could have been on another weekend. His son was coming Friday, and he didn't know what kind of reception he'd get or what his son's reaction to Olivia would be.

Friday afternoon, Clifton drove to the eastern shore to interview Harvey Cooper. The evenings were getting cooler by degree now, but the sun was out. Clifton depressed the electronic button to lower the windows.

The leaves had turned to a vibrant gold. The mixture of gold, rust, and green was an artist's paradise.

At five Clifton parked in front of Cooper's house and waited for a lawn service truck to pass by.

Cooper was kicking a soccer ball back and forth with his daughter. Clifton placed her at around ten. The man wore a green T-shirt and black shorts. The father and daughter had identical shades of blond hair, Cooper's cut short, hers gathered in a pretty fabric and elastic tie-back.

"That's it," Cooper said when he glimpsed Clifton. "Homework time."

"Ah, Dad," the daughter moaned.

"That was the deal." His tone brooked no argument, and she took the ball and moved slowly to the house.

Clifton greeted him and offered a business card. Cooper's reception was the exact opposite of Wheeler's. His nature was easygoing and calm, and he was eager to help.

"My wife told me to expect you."

"I understand that you talked to Lawrence's wife just before he died," Clifton said.

"I did." He shook his head in regret. "It was a sad occasion."

"Sally Palmer says that he tried to tell Ray something. Do you have any idea what it might have been?

He shook his head. "Every now and then, I still think about that night. And I haven't got a clue."

Clifton went through the same list of questions he used with each of the interviewees, alternating questions to suit the individual. Then he left the interrogator behind and switched the chat to a more relaxed topic.

"I understand you enjoy fishing."

"Do I ever." His eyes went soft. "The most relaxing pastime on earth."

They discussed his trips to Spednic and Moosehead Lakes in Maine. Apparently, his roommate from college had introduced him to the area.

Half an hour later, Clifton left, hoping to return home before Allen arrived.

Allen got there around six, just after Clifton put on the chili—Allen's favorite—that he'd fixed the night before to heat. He'd discovered that the flavor came through more if the chili was refrigerated for at least a night.

Allen's attitude was sulky at best. Clifton could tell

immediately that the weekend wouldn't be easy—maybe even a tough year.

"Let me help you with your bags," Clifton offered.

"I've got it." A younger version of Clifton grabbed his duffel bag and backpack and entered the house, glancing around. "Where to?" he asked.

"The basement. You get the couch in the rec room."

Clifton flicked on the light at the top of the stairs.

Veronica had asked if Clifton would rent her basement for a few months, giving her a chance to build her savings. She didn't want to rent to strangers.

The arrangement worked well for both of them, giving Clifton a chance to leisurely search for a house.

The basement consisted of a rec room with a hide-a-bed, a bedroom, and a bath. Clifton shared the kitchen with Veronica. When he or she felt like a decent meal, he cooked. Veronica wasn't much on cooking.

Allen dropped his bags beside the couch.

"How's school?" Clifton asked, opening the curtains on the tiny windows.

Allen shrugged.

So that's the way of things, Clifton thought. It was starting to be a tedious weekend already.

"Car working okay?"

"Yeah." Allen picked up the remote control, pushed the ON button to the huge TV that faced the couch. Then he flicked from channel to channel.

Clifton released an inaudible sigh. "Hungry?"

"Not really."

He searched for something else to say when he heard his sister walk across the floor above them.

She'd said she would stop by Giant's on her way home for ice cream.

She opened the basement door. "Cliff, Allen?" she called out just before her heels clicked on the stairs.

"We're here." Clifton said.

Allen stood, smiling for the first time since he'd arrived. "Aunt V!" He never would call her by her given name.

He met her near the stairs and gave her a huge hug, swirling her around and bringing squeals of delight.

A twinge of jealousy flipped through Clifton. He longed to share that easy camaraderie with his son. He wanted his son to pat his back, throw an arm across his shoulder in a roughhouse sort of way, and walk into the house with him, joking.

"My goodness. You've grown!" Veronica held him at arm's length.

Allen only smiled.

"And handsome, too. I bet the girls at Morgan are standing in line."

"Not quite." He laughed.

"I do know men your age love to eat. Cliff, that chili smells heavenly. I'm starved. Wash up, Allen, and we'll eat."

"Be right there." He proceeded to the bathroom.

Clifton waited a moment, trying not to let his impatience take over. It would take time and patience to win his son over. And he was short on both.

Bubbles surrounded Olivia, and lavender essence hovered in the air. She closed her eyes and leaned against the bath pillow. Olivia loved nothing better than a luxurious hour in the tub. She still had time to wash her hair, roll it, and get under the dryer in time to log onto the chat room Rochelle had taught her to use by ten that evening.

Her daughter's first sentence read, "Aunt Debra says you have a date tomorrow night. Who is this man?"

To which Olivia answered, "I don't have a date. One of my clients invited me to a family barbecue."

"According to Aunt Debra, the man has his eye on you. Do you like him?"

"He's okay," Olivia responded.

"Do you have the directions? Where does he live?"

"Near Debra. But he's picking me up," she scribbled quickly.

"Never, ever, let a man pick you up on a first date. From now on meet someplace neutral and public. That way if you need to get away, it's no problem. You've got your own transportation. Now you're stuck there, whether you like it or not."

"I can't very well leave a family dinner early. Remember, *he* didn't invite me."

"But he's picking you up, and he'll take you home. Not good."

"All right. When I'm on a first date, I'll drive."

"And meet at a neutral, public place."

"Yes."

"Mom, I'm going to type up some dating notes for you and e-mail it to you."

"That's not necessary, dear. I wasn't born yesterday."

"You're vulnerable because you've been out of commission for years. So what're you wearing?"

"I don't know. I'm still deciding."

"Make it casual and comfortable. Beige jeans, a shirt, and comfortable shoes. You don't want to look as if you're too interested. Keep him guessing. I know you. You'll wear one of those pantsuits that shouts 'I'm available.' "

Olivia laughed. "I'm not wearing jeans."

"At least make it casual, Mom."

They "talked" for another fifteen minutes and logged off. Olivia had trouble keeping up with typing, but this new way of communicating was great, especially since she could talk long-distance without it showing up on her phone bill.

Clifton heard Allen stirring in the next room at daybreak. He got out of bed, pulled on shorts and a T-shirt, and made a quick trip to the bathroom. Coming out, he went to the rec room to invite Allen to run with him.

Allen was already dressed in running clothes.

"Going for a jog?" Clifton asked.

"Yeah." Allen picked up a Walkman with earphones.

"Mind if I join you?"

He shrugged. "Suit yourself."

"There's a track just down the street."

"That's what Aunt V said."

They both did three minutes of warm-up stretches before they fell into step—first to walk and, once at the track, to jog. Allen stayed just ahead of Clifton the entire three-mile stretch. By the time they turned around and jogged one mile back, Clifton felt his age and slowed to a fast walk.

When he caught his breath, he glanced at his son. Allen listened to his Walkman, which was clipped to his shorts. "Want to tell me what's bothering you?"

At first Clifton thought that Allen hadn't heard him, but finally he asked, "Why does something have to be bothering me?"

"We haven't had a civil conversation since you arrived."

"Why do you keep bugging me? I don't bother you, do I?"

"You're my son. You're supposed to bother me." Clifton tried another tactic. "Are you angry with me for not being around?"

Allen took the earplugs off, let them dangle in his hand. "Listen, you had your own life to live, just like I have mine."

"I didn't want to be away from you, son. I didn't want you to leave."

"You didn't come after us either, did you?" He tightened his mouth as if he wished he hadn't said anything, put the earplugs on, and started jogging again.

Clifton picked up his pace to match Allen's, then put his hands on his son's shoulders to stop him.

"Is that what your mother expected? Is that what you wanted?"

His hands on his hips, struggling for breath, Allen shrugged with a devil-may-care attitude. "I don't want anything." Then he took off again, at a fast pace.

Clifton watched after him. He'd said the same thing

after Catherine left him and told him she wasn't returning. But he'd cared. *It tore me in two,* Clifton thought as he paced slowly back to the house.

Had Catherine's move been a test? Had she really expected that he'd pick up and move with her?

Clifton had assumed that she'd finished with the marriage, that the move was an easy escape.

And now his son had paid the price. Because he was alienated from Clifton, he'd felt abandoned. And the many times Clifton called him, all the paraphernalia Clifton purchased for him, couldn't take the place of an absentee father.

When Clifton made it home, Allen professed that he had to study. Clifton showered and drove to the homes around the scene of the heist.

The pulse of the neighborhood on Saturday morning was vastly different than midweek. He went to several homes and asked questions. Most people were reluctant to talk about it. They certainly weren't around when it took place.

In neighborhoods such as that one, with a park close by, at least children would have been playing in the area. But the parents assured him that they knew nothing.

The plan wasn't working out as well as Slugger had thought it would. The five thousand was almost gone—she only had one thousand left—and it had only been a month since she got the money from

Olivia. It wasn't her fault that she had to pay big bucks for everything. Information was always available—for a price.

Slugger had just paid a fortune to somebody who knew somebody who worked at a bank to find out where Ray Wheeler's money was stashed. It was nowhere near millions of dollars.

She snorted. Even with that nice cushiony job, he barely had a dime in the bank. She knew where the money was going. The fool. But one day he'd make a mistake, and she wanted to be there when he made it.

Now, she had a problem. Slugger couldn't wait until she was down to her last dime to get more money. And she wouldn't waste her time on some two-bit job when she could use her time more efficiently gathering evidence that would eventually put Ray away.

Back to the money. She didn't have any rich friends. But Olivia was rich. The woman would pay anything to protect her precious children.

She wouldn't actually do anything to Olivia's children, but Olivia didn't know that. Besides, Olivia was the only one she knew who had money to spare. It wouldn't hurt her to part with a little, temporarily. As soon as she got the reward money, Slugger would pay her back—every penny, plus interest.

She sealed the envelope and put a stamp on it. She drove to a mailbox situated in front of the post office and dropped the letter in it. She loved those drive-up boxes. No one would notice her wearing gloves on such a warm day.

* * *

Olivia scrutinized several outfits in her closet and discarded them. *What to wear?* she wondered as she selected another garment and held it up. Taking Rochelle's suggestions to heart, she refrained from the pantsuit, but jeans were out of the question. Her hips weren't the slim jeans shape.

The jeans Clifton wore Thursday had shaped his hips and molded his thighs. He was one virile man.

She wondered how many clients they were inviting tonight, then cast the thought aside. What she really needed to concentrate on was an outfit that made her full figure appear trim.

She really shouldn't have overindulged this week. But she hadn't gained more weight. That was some progress, at least. She'd also walked every morning, and a celebration was in order. She'd discarded the hot fudge cake with a scoop of ice cream topped with piping hot fudge and whipped cream. She patted herself on the back for walking by Godiva's without stopping.

Since eating a handful of a rich treat would defeat her purpose, she had to come up with something else to treat herself with. She wondered how the tradition of eating to celebrate began, and wished that the inventor had thought of something different, like a new dress or a trip. Maybe she'd get a massage and treat herself like a client. Then again, dinner with Clifton and his family would be a treat in itself—she hoped.

Veronica hadn't asked her to bring anything, but

Olivia used the invitation as an excuse to make a banana pudding that she'd craved for weeks.

Clifton arrived promptly at five. They had easy conversation on the ride from her house to his.

Olivia was unsure of how to interpret the hand lingering on her back seconds longer than necessary, sending searing hot licks of fire through her. She was glad he'd taken the bowl out of her hand. Otherwise, they'd have been scraping banana pudding off the pavement.

His son was as tall as he, but not as bulky. Gangly youth still clung to him, and he was just beginning to grow a few strings of hair on his chin. He was very polite, but restrained and watchful. Olivia readily detected that the easy camaraderie that existed between her and her children was missing with Clifton and Allen.

At evening's end, Clifton walked Olivia to her door and took her key, a departure from his usual smooth moves. Tonight he wanted to graciously take his lady home. Inserting the key, he opened her door. Suddenly they were both in the foyer.

She set her purse on a small table that fit under a huge gilded mirror. He slid the key beside the purse and took both of her hands in his. "Olivia, there's more than client and detective going on with us, isn't there? If I'm wrong, just say so."

Olivia took a deep breath, glanced at their joined hands and then at his magnificent eyes, struggling with her answer. Wasn't this what she'd wanted since she met him? "You aren't wrong," she finally said.

Clifton exhaled a pent-up breath. She wasn't denying it. "I know this is the worst possible time for us. I'm your employee, and I'm dealing with Allen's animosity toward me. But I hope you'll let me take you out. I want to get to know you better." He brought her hands to his mouth and kissed her knuckles.

She laughed. "You know I was just trying to decide how to approach you."

"No kidding?"

"Hey, my skills are rusty. My daughter told me that I approached this dinner all wrong. I was to drive myself to your place."

"But now that we have that first date over, we can breath a sigh of relief." Clifton wanted to stay longer, but he needed to get home to talk to Allen. He drew her to him, bent and kissed her lightly on the lips. Letting her go, he strolled to the door before he changed his mind and stayed.

Chapter 7

Allen's calculus book was open on the card table when Clifton returned from taking Olivia home. He glanced up when he saw his father.

"I don't know why you invited me here this weekend. You don't need me around to court your woman."

"Your aunt invited her. But while we're discussing it, I do like her. A lot."

"Yeah, isn't that great?" Allen said sarcastically. "You think you can carve out any more time with her than you did with Mom?"

"What the hell are you talking about now? You and your mother came first in my life, and *you* still do."

"Yeah, right."

Clifton sat on a stuffed chair. "We need to discuss what we started this morning."

He shrugged his shoulders in the negligent way

teens do. "Nothing's hassling me. Except I don't know why you invited me here in the first place. Did Aunt V initiate it?"

"You're my son, Allen. I love you very much."

"And you've certainly let me know that, haven't you?"

"In every way I knew how."

"Yeah, well, with efforts like yours I feel sorry for the kids of fathers who don't. Then, too, I couldn't tell the difference."

"Until you and your mother moved away I spent time with you."

"Really? Like playing catch with me like other fathers? Hell, most of the time I didn't even see you."

"I had to make a living for us."

"So did other fathers, but their kids saw them sometimes."

"We did things together."

Allen scratched his head. "Your memory of the past is a lot different than mine. I don't remember us doing much together. And when did you spend time with Mom?"

Clifton clamped down on his anger. He felt like saying she was the one who left. But using that argument would get him nowhere. After all, Allen grew up with his mother.

"What difference did it make? You weren't in our lives, anyway."

"I put a roof over our heads. I did the best I knew how." Clifton remembered the backbreaking hours. Sometimes he'd rubbed eyes gritty and red from lack of sleep, wishing he could nap, but he had to keep going, had to make the money to support their life-styles. He'd thought that by eighteen his son would understand.

"Oh, here we go again. Look, I don't want to talk about this tonight. I'm tired. I've got tests next week, and homework to finish. I've got to put all that money you're dishing out to good use."

"We need to air this. You need to under—"

"You need to understand that I've got school. You're paying enough for it." He turned a page in his text. "Maybe coming here was a bad idea."

"It wasn't. This is the first time anyone has said anything to me about this, and we need to talk about it."

Allen shrugged his shoulders. "It's gonna have to be later."

Rubbing his forehead, Clifton headed for his door. "I'll talk to you tomorrow, then."

"Yeah." Allen was already immersed in his work. Clifton wondered if his son could really be that deeply engrossed. Or was it all an act?

By the time Clifton woke Sunday morning, Allen had packed and gone.

There were no little telltale signs that he'd even been there. The hideaway was tucked in, pillows plump, the cocktail table pushed back in place. Sheets were in the washer. Not one little item, not even a stray pen or pencil, indicated that his son had spent the weekend in the next room—only the memory of their argument left unsettled.

* * *

Clifton jogged hard Sunday morning along the walking path bordering their neighborhood. He needed the exercise—needed to overextend himself. He'd been unable to sleep last night after the argument with Allen, which was why he hadn't heard him leave. Had he had a decent night's rest, he would have heard his son packing and slipping away during the early hours.

He'd never considered that winning Allen over would be easy, but the frustration from trying to figure out how to reach his son made him edgy.

The funny thing about life was that you couldn't rewind it like an inexpensive tape and start all over again. At the time, providing for his family had seemed crucial. He hadn't wanted his son to do without, as he'd had to do. He'd wanted his wife and son to live in a neighborhood and home they'd be proud of. He hadn't wanted children laughing at his son because he couldn't afford to replace shoes with holes worn in them. He'd wanted to buy his wife the furniture she desired, pretty dresses, curtains for her windows.

And he'd still lost them both, when she'd moved away. Many times he wondered if she would have stayed if he'd never worked that second job—or would she have felt that he'd failed her somehow, because he couldn't provide her with the trappings she desired? Would he have been enough? Had their relationship been stable enough? Perhaps she hadn't even desired the material things he felt driven to provide.

Clifton swiped a hand over his sweat-drenched face. Making the right choices wasn't easy. And trying to build from the wrong choices was even more difficult.

Clifton's next date with Olivia occurred the next week. Monday afternoon Clifton called, asking Olivia if she wanted to go to The Palace's happy hour after work.

"Sure." She hugged the phone against her ear, dropping her pen on the desk.

"I'll pick you up at five."

Olivia wore a hot pink, silk pantsuit with a black camisole. She dabbed on a little makeup and spritzed herself with a delicate perfume before he arrived.

"Sorry," he said once they were on their way. "Veronica overheard me on the phone and roped Bill into coming. So it'll be a foursome."

"That's fine." She'd enjoyed the group at the cookout. She did desire a little time with Clifton alone, though.

His hand tightened on the door handle. "She's got her eye on him, but he's not biting."

"Is that because they're working together, or is he really not interested? Because he looked like he was drawn to her at the cookout."

Clifton opened the door for her and she slid onto the leather seat. Rounding and entering the car, he picked up the conversation from where he'd left off.

"You can never tell with Bill. He was always hard to read in college. You'd think he hated a girl, only to find out later he'd pined for her all along." Clifton started the motor, backed out of the parking slot.

"He's definitely not ready to let Ronnie know. The man can think a situation through longer than anyone I know. Until he's done that, he won't make a move."

In just a few minutes they sat at a small, out-of-the-way table, where the music was at just the right volume for easy conversation. Veronica and Bill were already seated. She nursed a club soda while Bill drew on a draft beer.

Olivia greeted the couple. A waiter appeared, and she and Clifton ordered drinks—white wine for her, beer for him. They also ordered hors d'oeuvres. Debra had talked of coming here with dates, but today was Olivia's first visit. She always begged off for lack of time—there was always too much that needed doing.

Over chicken wings and celery sticks dipped in blue cheese sauce, the two couples joked, laughed, and began their journey toward a relaxing friendship.

Clifton locked his car and walked Olivia to her door. An inner sensation prompted him to look across the street when she inserted her key into the lock. It was dark in the house—the curtains drawn back, the blinds half open—but he sensed that the man was peering at them through the window.

When Olivia unlocked the door he followed her in, closing the door behind him.

"It was a lovely evening, thank you." She looked as if she were about to extend a hand for a shake.

"Don't thank me," he said, leaning against the wooden surface, regarding her. She resembled a deer caught in the headlights. "This is officially our second date." He stepped closer to her, grasped her hand, and pulled her to him, giving her plenty of time to pull back if she wanted to. "This means a good-night kiss."

She didn't pull back, but lifted her face to him. "Oh, yeah?"

He smiled. "Must have been that floppy hat, or those shades, or your softness, that took my breath away." His voice caught on the last syllable.

She went willingly when he pressed her against him. Her breasts crushed against his chest, the warmth searing through him. He readjusted his stance until her hips were flush with his. He lowered his head. His lips touched hers with a feathery stroke, and he caught the sigh that escaped her lips—the sigh that traveled to below his belt. "I've wanted to taste your lips since we met at that restaurant," he whispered.

"Then what are you waiting for?"

The smile left his eyes, replaced by unmistakable desire. Thrusting his tongue between her lips, he deepened the kiss.

She tasted like sweet ambrosia. Their tongues volleyed. He could taste her forever. The teaser had only whetted his appetite. He wanted more of her—to touch her all over.

Placing his hand on her back, he pressed her closer to him. Her softness drove him wild. He walked forward, forcing her to move backward until her back flattened against the wall and he moved his hips against hers—exalting in her womanly curves against his hardness. The moan that floated to his ears was like sweet music, and stirred his senses more than any woman had since . . . he couldn't remember when—didn't care. He only wanted to devour Olivia.

He hadn't expected to take this so far so soon. He'd planned to give her time to adjust to him. But then her hands inched under his jacket, playing a musical dance over his muscles. The contrast of her hands and her nails on his skin drove him out of his mind. Damn, he couldn't take much more of this. Sweat beaded on his forehead. He was only a step away from urging her upstairs.

He wanted to stay the night—to take this to completion—but it was too soon. Against his better judgment, he slowly eased his lips from hers and stepped away. He scrutinized her from head to toe. She looked like a glowing limp doll plastered against the wall.

He could barely stand on his own shaky legs. He ran an unsteady hand down his face. "It started out as a light good-night kiss."

She only nodded.

"Should I apologize?"

She shook her head.

He chuckled, lifted his right hand and traced it along her face, then lost his smile. "Cat got your tongue?"

"I think so." Her voice was smoky.

"I'd like to take you out again." He put his left hand against the wall, imprisoning her on one side.

She glanced away from him. "Are you sure that's wise?"

"Hell, I don't know. I don't always do the wise thing. I can only follow what I feel, and I need to get to know you better."

She was looking at him again. He stepped closer and kissed her lightly, then pulled away.

"But we're working together," she said cautiously, twining her fingers with his.

He blew out a long breath, bringing her hand to his lips, and kissed her palm. "I know that. And it goes against everything I believe."

She gazed at their entwined fingers, then focused on him. "I guess an outing won't hurt."

"Your enthusiasm is so encouraging." He straightened, but one arm still imprisoned her. "I'll call you." He dropped his arm from the wall, let her fingers go. Turning, he strolled to the door and opened it. Then he pivoted and faced her one last time.

"Did you know that the man who lives in the house across the street watches everything that happens?"

"Mr. Tompkins." She cleared her throat. "We call him the neighborhood watch. He's harmless enough. He doesn't go out much. He seems lonely."

"How long has he been here?"

"About six months."

He shrugged. "As long as you know." He let himself out into the night, the crisp air cooling him. He couldn't help glancing across the street again. Again, everything was dark, but he could clearly see a crack in the blinds at one of the windows that indicated a finger held the blind open in one spot. It was time he ran a check on Mr. Tompkins.

Olivia peeked through a tiny crack in the living room curtain. As Clifton drove off, she touched her fingers to her lips. Hot liquid still floated through her jittery stomach, and she pressed a hand there, hoping it would still the flutters, at the same time luxuriating in sensations she hadn't experienced in years.

What a kiss. What a man, she thought, still tingling with the play of his muscles against her fingertips, her hands. Why had she waited so long?

Olivia showered, using a honeysuckle-scented gel, and readied herself for bed. She sat at the French Empire desk, unable to concentrate on the accounting papers she'd promised Janice she'd go over. She might as well put them away. Then the phone rang. Thinking it was Clifton, she answered softly.

"Mom, Rochelle says you're dating."

It was Craig.

"There isn't a law against it, is there?" Laying her pen on her papers, Olivia slid from the chair and walked to the bed. Pulling back the gold spread with tiny rose flowers, she plumped the pillows and sat, leaning against the headboard, tucking her knees.

"Do you know anything about this man? When did you meet him?" he asked staccato fashion.

"Craig, I'm only dating him, not marrying him." She shouldn't let him get away with the third degree. After all, he was her child.

"But you're new at this. You knew Dad all your life, and you married him right out of high school. This is different. Things have changed. A lot. Boy, how times have changed."

"Uh-huh. But men are still the same. There are good ones, and those not so good."

"That's just it—you can't always tell the difference until it's too late. Do you need me to come home to check him out?"

"Of course not." He was taking concern for her too far. "I wasn't born yesterday, you know." To change the subject, she asked, "How is school?"

"Going fine. But Mom, I'm worried about you."

Olivia realized that not dating all those years was probably a bad idea. Her children had never seen her with men, and thought she was incapable of handling herself.

"Don't worry."

"What does he do for a living?" he asked

"None of your business. You're my son, not my father, young man."

"A *concerned* son. He does have a job, doesn't he?"

"Of course he does." Olivia sighed. "He's a private investigator."

"How did you meet him?"

Olivia shook her head. He was treating her as if *he* were the parent. *This is all new to him,* she thought indulgently. "His sister is a regular customer at the spa."

"Oh. At least you know someone in his family."

"I've met his son. He's a freshman at Morgan State."

"I guess he's okay. Rochelle and I looked him up on the Internet, but couldn't find anything."

Olivia bristled. "Why did you do that?"

"We wanted to make sure he was okay." There wasn't a hint of remorse in his voice.

"You are not to meddle, do you understand?"

He scoffed. *"You* always did."

"That's different. I'm your mother. I'm allowed."

She heard his long sigh. "We'll meet him Thanksgiving, at least."

"But not to give him the third degree. Understand?"

They talked a few minutes longer and disconnected.

Olivia glanced at the accounting papers across the room, scattered on her desk, and then at her watch. She wasn't going to get much done tonight. She'd work on them again after her morning walk.

Her children were going to have to get used to the idea of her with a date.

Olivia fingered through her mail—bills, credit card offers, second mortgage offers, a magazine, more junk mail, a letter with no return address. Suddenly a chill washed through her as she stopped at the white envelope.

Since the blackmail, mail with no return address made her cautious. She started to rip open the top and remembered that Clifton had said to handle the letter as little as possible. The envelope would already have many fingerprints on it, but the letter wouldn't. Still, a blackmailer would wipe the letter clean of fingerprints before mailing it.

Get a grip, she admonished, and berated herself for thinking the worst. The letter was probably just another advertisement. And she was carrying on for nothing.

Still, she rushed to the house, opened the door, and hastened to the kitchen, tugging on the silverware

AFFIX
STAMP
HERE

ARABESQUE ROMANCE BOOK CLUB
120 BRIGHTON ROAD
P.O. BOX 5214
CLIFTON, NEW JERSEY 07015-5214

Accepting the four introductory books for $1.99 (+ $1.50 for shipping & handling) places you under no obligation to buy anything. You may keep the books and return the shipping statement marked "cancel". If you do not cancel, about a month later we will send 4 additional Arabesque novels, and bill you a preferred subscriber's price of just $4.00 per title (plus a small shipping and handling fee). That's $16.00 for all 4 books for a savings of 25% off the publisher's price. You may cancel at any time, but if you choose to continue, every month we'll send you 4 more books, which you may either purchase at the preferred discount price. . . or return to us and cancel your subscription.

BOOK CERTIFICATE

Yes! Please send me 4 Arabesque books for $1.99 (+ $1.50 for shipping & handling). I understand I am under no obligation to purchase any books, as explained on the back of this card.

Name _____

Address _____ Apt. _____

City _____ State _____ Zip _____

Telephone ( ) _____

Signature _____

Offer limited to one per household and not valid to current subscribers. All orders subject to approval. Terms, offer, & price subject to change.

Thank you!

AN020A

THE EDITOR'S "THANK YOU" GIFT INCLUDES:
4 books delivered for only $1.99 (plus $1.50 for shipping and handling)

A FREE newsletter, Arabesque Romance News, filled with author interviews, book previews, special offers, BET "Buy The Book" information, and more!

No risks or obligations. You're free to cancel whenever you wish . . . with no questions asked.

3 QUICK STEPS
TO RECEIVE YOUR "THANK YOU" GIFT
FROM THE EDITOR

Send back this card and you'll receive 4 Arabesque novels! These books have a combined cover price of $20.00 or more, but they are yours to keep for a mere $1.99.

There's no catch. You're under no obligation to buy anything. We charge only $1.99 for the books (plus $1.50 for shipping and handling). And you don't have to make any minimum number of purchases—not even one!

We hope that after receiving your books you'll want to remain an Arabesque subscriber. But the choice is yours to continue or cancel, anytime at all! So why not take us up on our invitation to receive 4 Arabesque Romance Novels, with no risk of any kind. You'll be glad you did!

An important message from the ARABESQUE Editor

Dear Arabesque Reader,

Because you've chosen to read one of our Arabesque romance novels, we'd like to say "thank you"! And, as a special way to thank you, we've selected four more of the books you love so well to send you for only $1.99.

Please enjoy them with our compliments, and thank you for continuing to enjoy Arabesque...the soul of romance.

Karen Thomas
Senior Editor,
Arabesque Romance Novels

ARABESQUE

A PRODUCT OF

BET BOOKS

drawer. Using a dull knife, she carefully slid the letter out and opened it, laying the knife across it to hold it open. Dread sank into her as she read the familiar wording, the only difference being the location for the first phone call.

The blackmailer demanded another five thousand, or the evidence would be exposed.

Olivia fell into a chair and put her elbows on the table, rested her chin on her clasped hands, and shook her head. A mind-gripping anger dashed through her—she fought for control. She wouldn't pay another five thousand on top of Clifton's fee and the previous five thousand.

That was what this person would cost her. Twenty-five thousand dollars, at least.

She gripped the letter. She wouldn't stop until they found this creature. She tried to look at the positive side. This letter put her closer to finding the blackmailer. In a sense she was glad it had finally come. The waiting, the wondering, all took a toll. And Clifton hadn't found any hard evidence so far.

Olivia sighed. She'd hoped that Clifton would have made more progress by now. Carefully refolding the letter, using the knife, she grabbed a Glad storage bag, dropped the letter inside, and stuffed it all into her purse. Snatching her keys from the outside flap on her purse, she ran to the car and drove to Clifton's office.

Olivia Hammond didn't go out in public without flawless makeup and attire. When she arrived at Clifton's office minutes later, with her fresh scrubbed face, wearing jeans with splotches of dirt and a top several sizes too big—not to mention an old pair of walking shoes that should have been thrown in the trash long ago—Veronica did a double take and knew something must be wrong.

Olivia thought that reaction was because she was at the office—she'd refused to go there before. Now, after the arrival of the second blackmail attempt, pretenses were an unnecessary luxury.

Veronica was typing at her computer. Bill was talking on the phone. Olivia couldn't see in the other office.

"Is Clifton in?" she asked.

"I'll buzz him for you." Veronica picked up the phone and said a few words.

Clifton came out immediately.

"I . . . I have some news. I wanted to talk to you about it."

"Come on in. Can Veronica get you some coffee or soda?"

"No, no."

He led her to his office and closed the door behind them.

Olivia dug into her purse and handed him the letter. "It came in the mail this morning," she said. "I haven't touched the letter inside. I used a knife to open it."

"It's time to contact the police."

"No!" she shouted, then lowered her voice. "We can't do that."

"Come on over here and sit down." Putting a hand on her back, he led her to the chair facing his desk. Then he rounded his own desk and sat in his office chair.

"What are you afraid of?"

"For the children's sake, I don't want anything disparaging said about Joe."

"They're old enough to handle it. Besides, they aren't in the area."

"That doesn't matter. They still have friends here. And news of that magnitude will be blasted by the media from coast to coast." She sighed. "All their lives I taught them to do the right things because Joe and I always stood for right. We didn't steal, we didn't lie. We worked for what we needed. If I settle for the halfhearted effort the police made, and if they can't find who's doing this, then everything I've ever taught them will mean nothing." She shook her head. "No. I can't go to the police."

He blew out a long breath. It took everything he had not to go to her. But if he neared her, he wouldn't be able to think at all. He had to treat this as he would any case that came across his desk that wasn't fogged with the intimacy they'd shared. Yet, they had shared something special.

Still, he did leave his chair and round his desk. Sitting on the edge, he reached out and took her cold fingers in his own and rubbed them—offering her comfort—hoping his touch, while not sexual, would help her in some small way. "I'm not letting you go again. This time, I'll go in your place."

"I'm going."

"Damn it, Olivia."

"Don't curse at me."

"I'm not cursing at you. You're frustrating the hell out of me."

She straightened her shoulders, some of the starch

coating her voice. "I don't have a choice. Don't you see that?"

"There's always a choice. And you're making the wrong one." He dropped her hands and paced the small space, tugging at his tie, which all but strangled him. She looked so good without makeup, not all prepped up like she usually was. He guessed she hadn't thought about what she wore, an indication of how devastated she really was. Right then he wanted to take her to bed, and their relationship was nowhere near that point. With her state of mind, he couldn't make love to her, anyway, only comfort. But comforting was enough.

"You're only saying that because . . ." She cleared her throat.

"I'd say the exact thing to any client. The best alternative is the police. They can stake out the place, and possibly catch this person."

"Come up with something I can live with."

He sighed, ran a hand down his face. Leaning against the desk again, he didn't touch her this time. "I'll stake out the place. My eyes won't be off you for one second. This time you won't leave money."

"I agree."

"There's no sense in continuing to leave them money. Your children aren't being threatened at this point . . ." He stopped suddenly, raised thick eyebrows. "Did you say you agree?"

"Yes."

"All right."

Olivia half-tuned him out as he talked about tracking devices and other electronic gadgets.

She sighed. The next two days were going to be

the longest in her life. There were two sides to that equation, however. At least they were progressing. The blackmail letter was another clue to the equation.

Clifton watched the database disperse all kinds of credit card information about Tompkins. He'd put off researching that man long enough.

Tompkins had accounts with about a dozen different delivery services—mail order clothing, dry cleaners, groceries, medication. He'd even managed to find a doctor who made house calls.

Was he agoraphobic? Clifton made a note in his little book to ask Olivia if she'd seen the man outside at all since he moved in.

Clifton drove to the old garden apartment building in Laurel. A few people lingered outside, enjoying the late afternoon breeze. Children swung on monkey bars, slid down slides, rode high on swings, legs pumping in the air, and played catch.

Clifton found his way to Warren Jones's brother's apartment on the third floor. Warren was one of the robbers, who died a month after the heist.

Noise from a television turned to full volume spilled into the hallway. Clifton could smell fried chicken, and wondered if it tasted as good as his mother's. He hadn't had fried chicken in ages.

He rapped his knuckles against the door. Standing six feet, a man Clifton guessed to be about fifty answered. His dark brown beard, peppered with gray and neatly trimmed, gave him a grandfatherly appearance.

"Good evening. My name is Clifton Zayne."

"Yeah?" he asked, a puzzled frown marring his brow.

"I'm looking for Bobby Jones."

"You've found him."

"I'm a private investigator, and I'd like to talk to you about your brother, Warren." Clifton took a card out of his pocket and handed it to him.

Every one of Jones's fifty years showed on his face. Eyes dimmed with regret scanned the card. He handed it back to Clifton. "I don't know why. He's gone now. Can't you just let it be?"

"We believe that someone other than those who participated were involved."

Jones sighed, then stepped back to let Clifton enter the apartment. It looked as if he'd lived there for years. It was also rather neat for a man who lived alone. A well-worn recliner faced the television. The place needed a good dusting. But then, thought Clifton, so did his.

"Can you tell me anything about his friends?" Clifton asked, settling into the chair the man pointed to.

He sank into his recliner. "I don't know much about the bunch he ran with. I do know that he didn't have the sense to put together a robbery of that magnitude."

"What about anyone else he knew? Did he know anyone who worked with the armored car company?"

He shook his head no. "Warren was always looking for the easy way out. I can't tell you how many times

I tried to tell him that there wasn't an easy way, but would he listen?" He shook his head again.

"My client is being blackmailed."

"I'm sorry about that. But I can't help you there, either."

Clifton stood, pulled out his card, and gave it to him. "If you remember anything, give me a call."

He nodded and Clifton left, trying not to let his frustration get the best of him. He was well aware that investigating cases like this was like looking for a needle in a haystack. But the needle was somewhere out there. And if they were lucky it just might be the blackmailer.

He glanced at his clock. He'd drive to Olivia's. She might be home by now. Perhaps he could take her mind off her troubles.

Chapter 8

Olivia arrived at her shop at noon, but couldn't concentrate on work. By two she unlocked the front door to her house. She'd barely made it inside when Debra called, asking if she wanted to go out that night.

Olivia should have taken her up on the offer, but didn't. She wanted to spare her friend the worry. Debra had worried with her through enough problems to last a lifetime.

Debra talked a few minutes about a date she'd gone out on a few nights ago. The familiar tone of her voice and humorous description of the date soon had Olivia laughing, and for a few minutes she was able to put aside her worries.

Thank God for friendships, she thought as she placed the phone on the cradle.

* * *

"Remember, you must be aware of your surroundings at all times," Clifton said. "We'll be with you the entire trip. Just leave the bag and get out of there."

Olivia nodded. He'd gone over this a dozen times. "All right. I'll be fine. I was the first time."

"Don't forget. Drive back to your shop after the drop. I don't want you alone."

She nodded, feeling like a walking radio with all the electronic gadgetry they'd attached.

Clifton squeezed her in his arms before sending her off.

Olivia drove to the gas station. She had been told to pick up a package that was left there for her and read the instructions. She was instructed to drive to Camden Yards, to the Orioles game. She was to leave the money in a paper bag on the floor, against the wall, on the right side of the commode in the next to the last stall. She recited the seat number out loud.

"Olivia, drive just under the speed limit. Give us time to get there and get in position. Bill, you got a dress in your car?"

"Yeah."

"This is going to be a mess," Olivia said. "We're going to be in the tail end of rush hour traffic."

"You've handled it before, baby."

"Yes."

"Damn, whoever it is couldn't have picked a worse place. A tangle of people will be crowded into the stadium, making the situation tougher to monitor. And a ladies' bathroom at break." Clifton snorted, imagining the mile long lines hanging outside the door. "I don't like this. Why don't we scratch this? They'll call back."

"I'm not willing to take the chance," Olivia said. "At least this way, you have a chance to catch them. If we don't even try, we know we won't."

Bill was soon out of range, and they couldn't converse with him. Olivia drove to the park without incident, and since she was early, finding a parking space was easy.

Under normal circumstances, she'd have eaten a barbecue sandwich and gotten a drink before the game started. Now, her stomach was too jittery for her to even think of eating, and a dull ache started at her temple. She had an entire hour to wait before the game started, with nothing to do but worry.

Olivia watched the people around her, wondering if each person was the one who was blackmailing her.

The game finally started, and Olivia paid no attention to who scored, strikeouts, walks, or the roaring crowd surrounding her that stood and cheered. She'd only seen Clifton once since she arrived, and almost didn't recognize him in his Orioles hat and bomber jacket.

She'd yet to see Bill. Suddenly she remembered that Clifton had mentioned a dress. Was Bill attired in a dress? She glanced at the women around her to see if any stood six feet, well-built, with sleekly muscled shoulders and calves.

The image had Olivia chuckling for the first time in more than three hours.

She sighed. Wishing she could have worn jeans and comfortable sneakers instead of the uncomfortable heels and suit, she shifted in her seat, waiting for the seventh inning stretch.

The crowd was in a tear. Orioles vs. the Yankees brought out the fans in droves. Suddenly a roar burst forth, and everyone stood in unison. The dull edge of a headache blossomed full-blown.

Finally she proceeded to the rest room and stood in line. The place was packed, and more women fell in line behind her. Everyone had held on as long as they could. A five-year-old danced around with the urgent need to get to a stall. Someone let her cut the line.

Olivia understood the need to get children to a rest room quickly. Someday, Olivia thought, when women started designing more buildings, they'd make sure enough stalls were put in to accommodate large crowds of women. She'd yet to attend a convention—even at the best convention centers in the country—and not have to stand in a line between business sessions.

She snailed along for what seemed like forever before she made it to the requisite stall, opened her purse, and put the bag at the designated place. Flushing the toilet, she left the stall, washed her hands, made her way to her seat, and suffered through two overtime innings.

The crush of people leaving the park was staggering. Without seeming to be with her, Clifton followed her to her car, but she still hadn't seen Bill.

She got into her car and headed south on 95. In a few minutes, the cell phone Clifton had handed her rang.

"It was too crowded to tell who got that package,"

he said. "By the time Bill got there, the bag was still there but the contents were gone. You can expect another letter from them. I'll get to your house ahead of you and go in, so don't get frightened. I won't use any of the lights. Bill's going to follow you to your house. We'll be with you the entire time."

"All right. I hope we made the right decision by not paying that money." Hands clenched around the wheel, Olivia started the hour-long drive home.

Slugger was so angry she wouldn't have been surprised to see steam rising from her skin. Who the hell did Olivia think she was dealing with?

And here Slugger was trying to be nice, had even decided to pay her back.

Olivia had thousands of dollars packed away in the bank—just sitting there. Slugger knew this because she'd had her contact check Olivia's account, too. Olivia could afford to pay the money and not even miss it. But she didn't want to let even a little bit go.

Slugger stopped at another red light, picked up the package and fingered the couple of dollars on top of a bag lined with cut-up newspaper. She flung it across the car. It bounced on the window and fell to the floor.

A car horn beeped behind her. The light had turned green. She accelerated.

If Olivia wanted to play hardball, then so could Slugger. Olivia could have had it easy. But no. She was too cheap to pay the money. She'd learn to regret that decision. Slugger would teach her not to mess with her.

It didn't have to come to this. It was all Olivia's fault for being miserly.

Slugger drove from Baltimore to Rockville. She'd remembered Olivia's phone number long ago. She hadn't planned to call her. But Olivia had changed that.

A half hour after Olivia arrived home, she received the dreaded phone call.

"Do you think you can play games with me?" the caller said, obviously using a device that disguised voices.

"You don't have any proof, because my husband didn't commit a crime," Olivia bluffed. "I'm not paying you money."

"Well, if you don't care about your husband, what about your children? Rochelle's at Morehouse, and Craig is at Fisk. They're both highly accessible."

"You leave my children alone!" Olivia shouted, wishing she could hop through the phone and strangle the caller.

"You pay me my money!"

"You won't get away with this," Olivia hissed, clenching the phone.

"You better think about what's more important to you—your children, or your money."

Olivia fell silent, taking deep breaths.

"I want my money tomorrow. Get it by ten o'clock." She told Olivia where she'd receive the first phone call. Olivia picked up a pen and wrote the address on the pad. "And Olivia, wear a black dress and hat." The threat hovered in the air.

"I'll get you the money."

"You bet your sweet ass you'll get my money. Ten. And I'd better not see any cops. You got that?"

Olivia clenched her teeth. "Yes."

The phone clicked in her ear. Olivia dropped the phone and clutched her shaky hands together.

Clifton picked up the phone and dialed Star 65. He called his office and had Veronica trace the address.

Clifton held her in his arms. "Oh Clifton, my babies. I've got to get them, tonight!"

"Olivia, I'll get someone to watch your children." He dialed the office. Bill was waiting there. He instructed Bill to hire someone to guard the children while he dealt with Olivia.

"I have to know they're safe."

"You can't go there. Honey, you can't protect them. I'll see to that. It's time to go to the police."

"You heard him. They'll hurt my children if I go to the police." She shook her head frantically. "That's out of the question."

"Promise me you'll go to them after the payoff. Olivia, promise me."

She nodded. "I promise. As soon as my children are safe and with me, I'll go."

The phone rang. With shaky fingers Olivia picked it up, listened, and handed it to Clifton. The call had been made from a pay phone in Rockville.

Clifton got two personal protection specialists he knew in Atlanta and Nashville to protect Olivia's children.

She didn't sleep that night. The children called

Olivia, worried about her, every hour on the hour. Her son was packing a duffel bag, ready to camp out at the airport to catch the next flight home. It took fast talking to convince him to stay at Fisk. Clifton got on the phone and promised he wouldn't take his eyes off Olivia for one moment. He also had to recite his life's story, including present home and business addresses and phone numbers.

Saturday morning, Olivia applied extra makeup with a shaky hand. She wiped splotched mascara twice. Applying liner was out of the question. The bags under her eyes clearly showed her lack of sleep.

Determined to be the first one in line, she was at the bank fifteen minutes before it opened.

She hoped the teller or the surveillance camera didn't pick up on her tense demeanor.

"She didn't have to tell me to wear a black suit," she said to Clifton after she got the money.

"It's a scare tactic."

"It's midday on Saturday. I'll stand out."

"I'm worried about the shoes. You can't run well in them if you need to. If it comes down to that, kick the shoes off and run out of there."

Clifton handed her a pen-like object. "Clip this to your bra."

"Why?" She turned her back to him and clipped it to the inside center, where her grandmother used to tell her to hide her money.

"They're not for beauty. It's an audio receiving device. We can hear everything you say." He handed her another device. "Put this in your right ear. We can talk to you."

"All right." She inserted the device and he arranged her hair to hide it.

"Don't forget. Drive back to your shop after the drop. I don't want you alone." Most of what he said was a repeat from yesterday.

She nodded. "Yes, I'm going directly to the shop. We've talked about all of this."

He handed her a cell phone. "Stick this in your purse. Use this as a last precaution. Just push the recall button, and you can reach me. Your car is wired, so we can hear everything you say. With luck, you won't need the phone."

She walked to her car alone, drove to the phone booth at the gas station at Plaza Street—and waited.

There she got instructions to drive to another booth across town. Once she was on her way, she repeated her destination aloud so the others could hear.

Olivia arrived there in twenty minutes. The drive shouldn't have taken so long, but with all the lights and turns it wasn't as easy as it could have been.

At one point she glanced in her rearview mirror to see if Clifton was still with her, but didn't see his car when she stopped at a red light. "Clifton, I don't see you anywhere." She scanned the street through her rearview mirror, watching various vehicle makes and models, but she didn't see his or Bill's.

"You aren't supposed to see me," he said, exasperated. "I won't lose you. Just be careful. And don't talk, in case someone's watching."

The gas station this time was across an intersection on the right. She pulled into the station and parked near the pay phone. Just as she opened her door, the phone rang. She rushed to answer it and received another set of instructions. After copying them, she got into the car.

"I'm to blend in with a funeral procession at Westbend Cemetery. There's a bush near a tree where I'm to leave the money. I guess you'll have to watch me and join in with the procession."

"Good thing I wore a dark suit today," Clifton said. "I'll blend in just fine. I'm still with you, baby."

It took a half hour of chest-tightening Saturday driving to reach the graveyard. The procession, with car lights blazing, was already entering the grounds. Olivia turned on her lights. As always, there were slow drivers who left gaps in the traffic. Olivia slid into one of the gaps as if she belonged there. She followed the cars through an iron gate bedecked with two angels.

Once on the grounds, they passed three burial sites already in progress. It was a busy day for funerals, and seemed to take forever to get to the one where she was supposed to appear.

Finally the hearse stopped, and cars parked along the curb of a freshly dug grave. Olivia parked her car and sat there, observing the area as others exited their vehicles.

Women gathered the flowers. The pallbearers lifted the expensive casket out of the hearse and carried it to a green tent with two rows of chairs placed on green carpeting. They set it over the grave.

The family exited the limousine and made their way to the tent.

A lump formed in Olivia's throat. She hated funerals. A deep regret tightened her chest.

A young woman dabbed at her eyes with a linen handkerchief and leaned on a man's shoulder. His arms were wrapped securely around her.

Olivia thought of Joe, traveling back twelve years. A tear slid down her cheek. She pulled out a tissue from the minipack she stored in the door pocket, sniffed, and dabbed at her eyes.

"Get yourself under control, girl," she said.

"What's going on, Olivia? Come on, baby. Stay with me. Don't let this throw you. I'm here. You're not alone. The children are safe."

His low familiar voice calmed her by degrees. She breathed deeply.

"Olivia?"

"I'm okay," she said, pulling down the visor. Her makeup was a mess. Opening her purse, she retrieved her compact and dabbed powder on her face, repairing the damage.

"See the tree to the right of the grave?"

She glanced out the side window. A tree and low bush stood several yards from the grave.

"I see it."

She waited several minutes for everyone to exit their vehicles and convene at the graveside. When the last straggler stood on the outskirts of the crowd, Olivia finally exited her car and shut the door quietly.

She put the straps of the oversize black purse over her shoulder and walked near the designated tree, just a few feet from the last row of mourners.

The minister prayed. Heads bowed. Sniffles mingled with the minister's words. Women leaned forward, trying to keep their heels from sinking into the earth.

Easing the large black cosmetic case out of her purse, she slipped it under the bush, then silently tiptoed to the back of the crowd. The minister finished the prayer and offered his final comforting words. Olivia studied the faces to see if she recognized anyone. She didn't.

When the minister asked the group to reassemble at the fellowship hall at the church to commune with the family and for refreshments, Olivia joined the others as they returned to their vehicles. A few people lingered, consoling the family. As soon as a space cleared, Olivia drove away.

Wearing dark shades, Clifton lingered at the grave, a little off to himself in a perfect spot to view the bush where Olivia stored the bag stuffed with folded newspaper. He wanted to watch her, instead, but he didn't dare take his eyes off that bush. At least people didn't crowd it to the point that he couldn't see. Two people neared it, but didn't stop.

One woman wearing a spiffy black dress that touched just above her knees and a sassy black hat stopped near the bush and glanced around. She dropped her purse, bent, and unobtrusively picked up the cosmetic case with her purse and slipped the case inside. She then walked swiftly to a gray Nissan and pulled away.

"Bill. Follow the woman driving a gray Nissan." He rattled off the license number and, just in case someone was still watching, he casually strolled to his car.

"She's coming through the gate now," Bill said a few minutes later. "She's turning left on Cedar."

Clifton started his car and followed the directions that Bill rattled off. He dialed the office on his cell phone and gave Ronnie the plate number to look up in the computer database.

Minutes later, she said, "It belongs to a Chandra Smith, address thirty-four hundred Chase Street, apartment seven twenty."

"She's headed in that direction," Bill said. "This is too easy."

"Either she's an amateur, or the plates are stolen." By now they were on the Beltway driving toward Laurel.

As Olivia drove in the direction of the spa, the reception was cracking up. She was quickly going out of range. She did hear thirty-four hundred Chase Street, and the apartment number, and snatches of conversation between the men—thirty-four hundred Chase Street seemed familiar, somehow. "I know that address, but I can't remember why," she said to Clifton.

"Could be someone you know, or who was involved with the heist. We'll see you at the spa, Olivia. The reception's breaking up."

At the red light, Olivia made a U-turn and headed toward Chase Street. No way was she going to her office, biting her manicured nails, waiting for a phone call from Clifton. She would look the blackmailer in the eye. She had every right to do so.

She had a burning need—a driving desire—to know who threatened her children and had stolen from her twice. Clifton couldn't deny her that.

They had exited the Beltway. At the red light, Clifton shoved off his dress shoes and pants, leaving on his shorts. At the next light he struggled into his sneakers, making quick work of tying the laces in the cramped space. He then had to rub a crimp out of his shoulder. When the light turned green he accelerated, and he unbuttoned his shirt and cuffs while steering. Within five minutes, he'd shrugged out of his jacket and dress shirt, leaving on a black T-shirt. Sweat trickled between his shoulder blades.

He felt into the backseat for a well-worn fishing cap that lapped over his ears. Watching the signs, he followed the Nissan into the apartment complex. Quickly, he maneuvered into the parking space across the drive from where she parked. At the last minute he remembered to throw the shades onto the passenger seat and snap on his fanny pack. His .38 was tucked inside. Then he exited the Taurus, looking as if he were just returning from the gym.

Bill was already in a hiding spot on her floor.

Jauntily and with a low hummed tune, the woman entered the secured building, holding the door for Clifton to enter behind her. Clifton thanked her kindly and held the door for her. He followed her to the elevator. They were the only ones who entered.

"What floor?" she asked in a friendly voice, holding her keys in her right hand.

"Seventh," Clifton said, facing the door. Once it closed, he stood in the left corner. She stood in the right corner, humming. She was an attractive sister, Clifton thought. Slender and tall, about five-eight, too thin for him, but she was a looker. Not everyone was as foxy in a short, curly hairstyle. Her high cheekbones on her oval face, which barely held any makeup, were perfect for it.

Then Clifton noticed her clothing. The black dress was pretty, but inexpensive. The same for her shoes. They looked as if she'd purchased them from Payless. They definitely weren't designer-quality leather. Her earrings and the necklace that curved around her neck were bad-quality fake pearls.

Her long neck and legs would definitely appeal to many men—long—long legs just the right size, not too skinny, and not too large. Her slim, hourglass shape would curve perfectly to a man's hands. But he'd take Olivia's warmth any day. Winter would be closing in fast, and Olivia's snugly softness would keep him warm and contented. And damn if she couldn't cook. He was getting tired of his own cooking and McDonald's.

It was only recently, after meeting Olivia that meaningless affairs had grown even more unattractive to him.

He wondered at the woman's connection to Olivia, and her motive.

The elevator stopped on the fourth floor and three teenage girls entered, wearing identical shorts and T-shirts. One pushed the eleventh-floor button and they talked incessantly about some boy one of them was intrigued with.

Finally, the elevator stopped at the seventh floor. Clifton held the OPEN button as she exited. He followed her out, keeping several yards behind her.

As she inserted her key in the lock, he saw Bill closing in from the opposite direction. She opened the door and Clifton grabbed her arm and pushed her inside, holding one hand over her mouth. Bill entered behind him. She struggled fiercely against his constraint.

"Hold it right there!"

The voice cut off the woman's shriek.

"What the hell?" Almost losing hold of the woman, Clifton glanced to the left and watched Olivia bouncing down the hallway, swinging her black purse and still wearing her heels. Winded, she made her way to the door.

"Go on in," she said.

Clifton tightened his hand across the woman's mouth and held her arms tightly against her body under her rib cage. A thick black heel knocked into his leg.

"Damnit." He struggled with her into the apartment and pushed her into a worn chair. "Lady, you've got some explaining to do."

Her attention wasn't on him. It had transferred to Olivia, whose chest rose with labored breaths.

"Chandra?" Olivia asked, a frown marring her forehead, storm clouds gathering in her eyes. Olivia bent and picked up the purse that had dropped on the floor. She opened it and retrieved the cosmetic case.

With a hand on her back, Bill urged her into the apartment and closed the door behind them.

For a moment, Olivia looked as if she would faint. Then she locked her knees. "It was you blackmailing me?" A mixture of astonishment and hurt mingled in her voice, just before she sailed across the floor. Clifton let Chandra go and caught Olivia's fist just before it made contact.

Chandra scurried away. Bill caught her and handled her into a ragged chair.

Clifton had one arm around Olivia's waist to restrain her. She had seemed such a docile type, too. But you didn't mess with a sista's babies.

"Just settle down, will you?" Clifton shouted.

"I'm not settling nothing. Let me go!" she shouted between clenched teeth.

He muffled an oath. His worst experiences in police work were with two women going at each other.

He tried to talk to her. Getting her to cooperate long enough to get her in the chair without hurting her was out of the question.

"Either you settle down or I'm dragging you out of here," he hissed.

She glanced at him, tightened her lips. "You wouldn't dare."

"Try me."

"Fine." She breathed deeply. Clifton urged her to the chair Chandra had vacated, but she wouldn't sit. "I'm not going to do anything. You can let me go."

"Why?" she asked, staring at Chandra.

The younger woman looked away, unable to meet Olivia's eyes.

"Who is she?" Clifton asked, rubbing his throbbing leg. He wanted to throttle the woman.

"She was my receptionist. She just quit." Her mouth tightened around the words. "Now I know why."

Clifton tightened his arms around her for comfort. Olivia wasn't accustomed to other people doing for her. She probably didn't even realize he was there. First he'd deal with the problem at hand.

"Who is watching my children? I want names, phone numbers, and addresses."

"No one."

Olivia took two steps toward her. Chandra pressed against the back of her seat.

"Don't mess with me," Olivia said in a crisp voice usually reserved for her children.

"It was just me. I—I knew mentioning your children would bring you around. It was just an empty threat. I wouldn't actually do anything to them."

Olivia started for her again. Clifton restrained her.

"I've got to call the police. Stay put," he said, giving her a light squeeze before he left her side.

"The police?" Chandra shouted. "But nobody got hurt. I didn't even use a gun."

"Lady, you committed all kinds of crimes in the last month, and extortion is just the beginning."

"But I wasn't going to hurt anyone. I just wanted to find out who planned that robbery. I don't want to go to jail," she wailed.

"Who's working this with you?" Clifton asked.

"No one." She looked nervously from Clifton to Olivia.

"I don't believe you," Olivia said.

"It's true."

"Tell us about this evidence," Clifton said.

She gazed down at her hands and tightened her jaw before staring at them again. "There is none. I don't know who pulled that robbery."

"Why Olivia?" Bill asked.

The younger woman glanced away and then back at Olivia. "Because you had it to give."

"I didn't have a dime to give."

"I . . ." Then Chandra sighed. "I just want to find out who planned that robbery years ago. Who talked my dad into doing it. He . . . he died there." She glanced at her watch, twisting it on her arm.

"Who was your dad?"

"Jonas Potts. He mailed my mother a letter. I found it a few months ago. It said that his ship had come in, and that everything was going to be all right with them. That he'd soon be able to marry her. You see, she wouldn't marry him because he didn't have a stable job. He was always going from one job to another—none of them paying much. Mom told him that until he settled down she didn't want anything to do with him."

"Do you have the letter?" Clifton asked.

"It's in my bedroom."

"Get it. And don't try anything."

"It's a little late for that, isn't it?" The spirit she struggled for fell flat.

Clifton gave Olivia a gentle clasp. "Don't do anything while I'm gone."

He and Bill flanked Chandra as they walked to the only bedroom in the apartment. A wooden plaque with a baseball signed by Hank Aaron mounted on it held center place on the dresser. *Slugger* was written on the brass plate beside it.

Chandra opened the drawer of an old, scarred bedside table and extracted a bible. She took the letter out and handed it to Clifton.

The writing on the envelope was dated three weeks before the heist. He knew that date by memory now. Clifton took the letter out of the letter-size envelope and glanced up. "Let's go back to the living room."

When they returned, Olivia stood by the window, gazing out. The room overlooked a small grove of maples and oaks. Under them sat picnic tables and playground equipment.

Chandra sat in the same chair she'd vacated. Again, Clifton and Bill flanked her.

Clifton read the letter. Indeed, Potts had written that his ship had come in. No more slinging hash for Norma. No more hard times. This time would be different from all the others. This time, he had an inside track.

Clifton came up behind Olivia and handed her the letter. Quietly, she read the contents and returned it to him, without comment.

The question is, Clifton thought, *who was the inside track? Was it one of the managers? Was it Joe? Who?*

Finally Olivia turned. "How much of my money is left?" she asked.

"About a thousand."

"I want it. Right now."

"Olivia? The agreement was that we call the police."

She sighed.

Chandra looked hopeful. "There's a reward. I just want to know. You can have it."

"The reward can't replace my peace of mind. It can't bring back my husband, or your father. And whatever you believed didn't give you the right to steal from me or threaten my children."

"I—"

"You'd better stop while you're ahead," Bill said.

Clifton and Bill flanked Chandra again as she went to the bedroom. She reached inside the same drawer and pulled out the bills. She handed them to Olivia.

Olivia counted every cent. She already had the cosmetic case in her hand. She took the money out of it, depositing it in her purse.

Then she dug into her purse, pulled out a small pad of paper, and wrote a note. It was a promissory note stating that Chandra Smith owed her four thousand two hundred dollars, plus interest, plus expenses, and would make payments each week. Chandra also had to sign a statement admitting to her crime, which Bill had hastily written.

Chandra balked. "But, I don't have a job right now. I was living off that money." She pointed to the money in Olivia's hand.

"Then you need to get a job, don't you? A smart woman like you should be able to in no time. It's either that, or the authorities. And I wouldn't advise you continuing in this line of work. Next time you won't get off so easy."

"Easy? I've got to work two jobs to pay all that back. I can't find that man if I'm working night and day."

Olivia took a few steps toward her.

Clifton thought he'd have to restrain her again. He was getting damn tired of that.

"Your mother tried to force your father into assuming responsibility before she would marry him—before he could influence you," Olivia said. "That was why she wouldn't marry him. She didn't want you to grow up in that atmosphere and repeat his mistakes. Your father made a choice that he paid with his life. That your mother paid for. That you paid for. And the women whose husbands worked at Town Securities.

"You made a decision that you have to pay for, that I'm *not* going to pay for. You *will* pay my expenses for this incident, and if it's going to take two jobs for you to do it, you're going to work those two jobs, or else."

The threat hovered in the air. Clifton heard a door slam, children running into the hallway.

"What have you discovered so far?" Clifton asked her in the ensuing silence.

Lips tight, Chandra sighed, shaking her head. "Nothing much. I copied newspaper articles and started following people. Ray Wheeler is gambling again. Just small stuff." She pleaded with them. "I've got to be able to follow him. You've got to make her understand."

"How do you know he's gambling?" Clifton asked. He ignored her last plea.

"He and my dad used to gamble together. I knew their hangouts."

"Which are?" Bill had stood quietly so far.

Olivia went through the kitchen, opening the refrigerator, freezer, and cabinets.

"A place on Cabaret and Reign in St. Mary's. It's

a private party, mostly Tuesday night poker. I can't get in, but I've seen Ray there."

Clifton jotted the info on his pad.

"My dad paid with his life. Why should someone live off that money when so many people died? Or just throw it away, the way Ray Wheeler does?"

"My husband died, too. He didn't deserve to die and leave his two children and wife behind."

"Somebody planned that robbery, and I want to know who," Chandra said.

"You don't know any more than we do. And it doesn't excuse the fact that you threatened my children."

"You're rich. You own that nice spa. You have plenty of money. Why were you trying to be so cheap?"

Olivia was across the room and on her like a shot. Clifton couldn't restrain her before she smacked Chandra with the full force of her anger.

Chandra reeled, bringing a hand to her cheek.

Bill jumped back.

Clifton caught Olivia just before she went down for business, and he dragged her across the room.

"Feel better now?"

She blew out a breath. "Lots." She dusted her hands together. Then, when she realized what she'd done, she slid into a seat.

Olivia was appalled. She'd never hit anyone in anger before. She never got into fights in high school. She never lost her control.

She should realize Chandra was young and naive. It was almost like talking to a child—except that her children weren't that naive. She'd trained them not to be as uninformed, as she'd been when she married.

Quietly she said, "I worked for what I have. I'm not rich." She fought for control. How could she tell a twenty-two-year-old the kind of work and mind-numbing fear that went into getting where she was? Sure, she was comfortable, but she wasn't rich. Suddenly, Olivia was too tired to even try to explain. "I'll meet you at your office, Clifton." She took a few bills out of her purse and placed them on the table. She walked to the door, turned the doorknob, and faced Chandra. The younger woman clutched her jaw.

Clifton eyed Olivia warily as he walked to the freezer to make a makeshift icepack.

"Let me know the minute you get a job. And it had better not take long." Olivia opened the door and walked out. She wouldn't let her starve, but she wouldn't pay her more money, either.

Chapter 9

By the time Clifton made it to the office, Olivia had plopped on the sofa with a cup of Veronica's coffee and had slipped her feet out of her tight shoes. As soon as the door opened she unobtrusively slipped her feet back into the heels. She needn't have.

Veronica eased into Clifton's office and shut the door when she recognized the storm clouds on his face.

Trying not to get distracted by graceful calves and well-turned ankles, he paced over to Olivia, leaned over her with his hands on his hips. He still wore the shorts and T-shirt. "What the hell did think you were playing at? What if more people were in that apartment? More than we could have handled with you in the middle of it all? What if they had guns?" His voice started low, but quickly increased in volume and intensity.

His posturing didn't faze Olivia. She answered him calmly. "I wanted to see who was blackmailing me. I told you that address seemed familiar."

"But I told you to go to the spa, where you'd be around other people for safety."

"I'm not a child, Clifton."

"You acted like one."

She raised an elegant eyebrow. "You're stepping over the line."

"Woman."

Olivia tilted her chin, crossed her arms under her breasts, pulling Clifton's eyes to her roundness. "Everything turned out just fine. All your dire predictions didn't happen, so you might as well sit and relax."

Tearing his focus from her breasts, he took a moment to remember why he was ranting. Then he paced, veering between frustration and anger.

Olivia let him blow off some steam. Men had a tendency to do that. That smack had gone a long way toward easing the tight fist in her chest.

After he'd paced a while he sat beside her, taking her hand in his own, and blew out a deep breath. "How are you?" he finally asked.

"I'm angry, but fine."

He squeezed her hand. "Well, at least it's confirmed that it was an inside job."

"What's next—"

The office door burst open. A young man and young woman walked in, flanked by two muscled men wearing almost identical sports jackets.

Clifton stood.

"Mom! You okay?" they asked in unison. They ran

to her, scanning her from head to toe. The young man stood at Clifton's height. The young woman was a thinner version of Olivia. They wore jeans, with shirts and blazers.

Olivia stood and opened her arms to them.

The muscled men ambled to Clifton and shook hands. "Couldn't hold them back."

"What are you doing here? I distinctly remember telling you to stay put," Olivia said, her smile belying her stern tone as she held them close.

"We couldn't. Not with you in danger," Craig countered, frowning at his mother.

"I can take care of myself."

"You got that right." Clifton sank into the couch. "I had to tear her off Chandra."

"Clifton," Olivia warned. Her cheeks warmed prettily.

"Shrieking like a banshee, whipping the daylights out of Chandra."

"Mom!" Two mouths hung open.

"Had a regular alley cat on my hands."

"You cut that out right now, Clifton Zayne." She glared at him, wagging a finger.

Clifton held up both hands. "Yes, ma'am."

Craig focused on Clifton for the first time, his frown pulling his eyebrows into a V. "What's Chandra got to do with this?"

"She's the blackmailer."

"Chandra?" Rochelle asked. They knew the employees at the spa, as they'd both had to work there from time to time. Olivia believed in teaching her children about the business and had doled out small chores around the shop for their allowances. Of course, now they held regular full-time summer positions there.

"But she works for you," Rochelle said.

"Worked. She quit just after you left."

They pulled up chairs. "How long has this black-mailing been going on?" Craig asked.

Clifton and Olivia spent the next hour bringing them up to date on the blackmail and his role.

They sat in Clifton's office with cups of cold coffee that no one was drinking. Craig and Rochelle had left for home, and the muscled men were at the airport awaiting their departure flights.

"Do you believe Chandra?" Olivia asked.

"Yeah." Clifton glanced at her and nodded. "I don't know why, but I do."

"I want my money back. Every cent. It makes me so furious that she thinks the end justifies the means."

"You'd be surprised at how many people feel that way."

"She'd never consider that businesses have expenses. Wages. Benefits. Rent. Insurance. Accounting. Supplies. And the list goes on. I'm a long way from rich."

"She has no idea of what's involved in running a business. Some do, which is why they never attempt it in the first place. She's young."

"And that excuses her?"

Clifton shook his head. "The question is, where do we go from here? We have the blackmailer. Do you want to leave it at that?"

"I still want the person who's responsible for my husband's death caught."

"All right. We'll add the information she gave us to what we already have. You go home and relax. I'll focus on the employees, including Wheeler. A few have been eliminated already. They don't seem to have the patience to wait to spend that money. They would have flashy cars, and a flashy house. They'd have spread it through the whole neighborhood, and wouldn't have been able to lay low for twelve years. I'm thinking we're looking for someone who was living an average middle-class or upper middle-class lifestyle before the robbery, and still is."

"Well, I'm going home."

"I'll walk you to your car."

Olivia waved to Veronica and Bill and walked with Clifton to the elevator and to her car. They stood there a moment talking small talk.

He took one of her hands in his and rubbed the back in delicate strokes.

"Dress in your prettiest dress tomorrow night. I'm taking you out."

"We have nothing to celebrate. Clifton—"

He put his finger to her lips. "We're going out. I'll start again tomorrow morning. We're still hyped from this afternoon." He kissed her briefly on the lips. No long lingering kiss this time. "First dinner, then dancing. I get to innocently hold you in my arms. And the clubs won't be packed," he assured her.

Olivia's expression softened. "All right."

"Go home to your children."

"Stop by later on. If you have time."

He smiled. "I'll make time."

Clifton drove them to Archer's, a seafood restaurant east of Annapolis. He'd called ahead for reservations, requesting a table overlooking the water. Private boats, both sail and motor, were docked, their owners enjoying the last of the weekend and the last few weeks of decent weather.

The sun was just about to set, its reflection shimmering on the water, fading slowly away, by the time they opened their menus. Olivia hated to glance at her menu for fear she'd miss a rare moment of the view. She scanned it quickly and ordered the seafood combo.

They shared a shrimp cocktail. Even though she loved to eat, Olivia didn't think she could eat an entire appetizer with her meal.

When the meal arrived, Olivia knew she'd need a doggie bag before it was all over. The food looked and tasted delicious.

"Veronica tells me you're from Cleveland. Why did you move here? Was it to be near your son?"

"Two reasons. I wanted to spend time with Allen, and Bill and I were college friends. He made me an offer."

"Where did your son grow up?"

"He and his mother moved to Atlanta five years ago. Six months later she filed for a divorce." Clifton had been bitter about that for a very long time.

"I'm sorry."

"I was pretty bitter about it, but lately I've come

to terms with it. I thought the marriage was just like any other normal marriage. And then suddenly she received a job offer and was gone."

"Oh, Clifton."

"If the marriage had been stronger, if I'd taken more time out for her, then things might have been different. But you know that fear men have of providing for everyone. My priorities were skewed."

"But you missed your son." Olivia placed her hand over his for a second.

"He's here now, and that's what counts. Actually, Allen and I are joining Bill and Veronica at an Orioles game tomorrow." Clifton sipped his wine. "One of his clients gave Bill four tickets. They're out of town and can't use them. Do you like baseball, Olivia?"

"I'm not a real enthusiast, but my son loved the sport, so the three of us, Rochelle, Craig, and I, went to see the occasional game at Camden Yards—at least one a season after he turned fourteen. It kind of grew on Rochelle and me. Especially since she got to eat hot dogs, peanuts, and all the popcorn she could handle."

"Do you watch the games on television?"

She shook her head. "I never could watch sports on TV."

Clifton laughed. "I wish I had another ticket."

"You need the time with your son. And," she said, spearing a shrimp, "I'm predicting the Orioles will win."

"I'd take you up on that if the Cleveland Indians were playing, but since they aren't, either team will do."

"You traitor. You're a Marylander now. Where is

your loyalty?" Her smile faded. "After Friday night, I'm not ready for another game."

It was his turn to offer her comfort. "You've got great children, Olivia."

She smiled. "I think so."

"You raised them well. They want to care for you now."

"I tried so hard to let them be children. I didn't want Craig to feel he had to take on Joe's responsibilities. I always stressed that."

"But now he's a man, and he thinks like one. So you've done your job well."

Olivia shook her head, a small smile escaping. "Where has the time gone? Only yesterday they were babies."

The conversation led to their favorite movie, favorite books and foods.

Olivia discovered that she couldn't eat as much with Clifton as she could when alone because they spent the time talking. She had enough left over for tomorrow's dinner.

Clifton insisted they share a hot fudge cake with ice cream topped with melted chocolate and whipped cream. He pushed the dish between them and dished up the first spoonful for her, holding the spoon to her mouth.

"I'll have to walk an extra twenty miles because of tonight."

"Do you walk often?"

"Usually every morning. I cheated for weeks after my children left. My daughter usually walked with me, and it was difficult doing it alone. At the same time, I suffered with the empty nest syndrome."

"I walk every morning, too. Maybe we can walk together sometime."

"I think I'd be too slow for you."

"I walk, jog, then walk again. Most of the time, we'd be together."

"Well, maybe we *can*. Sounds like fun." The kinship they shared warmed Olivia.

For so long, Olivia had wanted a companion to walk with. And now, finding it had been that easy. She smiled at Clifton across the table as she took another spoonful of dessert. It was odd how when you least expected it, something special and unexpected could happen. A walk with someone might seem like such a small thing, but to Olivia it meant the world. For years she'd done everything alone. Now, to have someone who thought she was special, even though she was still thirty pounds overweight, left Olivia speechless and with a sudden warmth flowing through her.

Veronica dressed in a new pair of jeans for the game, and what she called a mauve cashmere sweater that, according to her, *went well with her coloring*. The sweater had a deep V neck that Bill appreciated. Clifton hoped she didn't catch a chill while trying to impress him. He shook his head. The changes women went through amazed him.

Clifton had the idea that Allen might turn the invitation down, but being an avid baseball fan he couldn't pass up a chance to see the Braves and Orioles together. He certainly wouldn't come just to be with his father.

Camden Yards was smaller and more intimate than

many stadiums in the league. They wouldn't need the binoculars this time, since their seats were situated right behind home plate, nearly eye level with the players.

Earlier, on their way back from getting sandwiches from Boog's Barbecue, Clifton had caught a ball that Albert Belle hit into the stands during practice. He'd given it to Allen, who was thrilled to have it.

Still, Allen had talked more with Veronica and Bill since they'd arrived—in plenty of time to see the start of the game.

They'd even walked partway around the upper deck to the concession area, to view the skyline. Clifton was unfamiliar with most of the landmarks. Bill pointed out Harbor Place, where they'd have dinner after the game, and other landmarks.

Allen balled up the wrapper from his sandwich and sipped his Pepsi.

"Allen, let's take the trash to the can." Bill and Veronica passed their trash to Allen, and Clifton walked with his son down the aisle. After they dumped it, Clifton urged Allen to take a stroll. They still had time before the game started. People were quickly entering the stadium, searching for their seats.

"I've been thinking about our conversation the other night. Maybe I should have come after you and your mother. I was hurt, but I shouldn't have let it get in my way."

Strolling slowly beside him, Allen tucked his hands deep into his pockets and remained silent and stiff.

"I think this happens when couples don't talk to each other. Sometimes we get so caught up in work that we let the relationship—the most important thing—slide. We just think our families will always be there, and forget that we have to work at the relationship just to keep it alive.'' Clifton put a hand out to stop his son and looked him straight in the eyes. ''I wish I had done it differently. But I never stopped loving you. There wasn't a day that went by that I didn't miss you, son.''

Allen turned his back to Clifton and rubbed a hand over his head. He sighed deeply.

Clifton put a hand on his shoulder and squeezed, realizing that Allen still needed time. Five years of hurt, anger, and resentment weren't going to disappear in a week, or even a month. They strolled quietly back to their seats just before the players appeared on the field.

On Monday morning Clifton typed the weekly report for Olivia. He also revisited the data on employees. The motive was the key—possibly gambling, for Wheeler. He couldn't wrap his finger around Cooper's motive yet, except that he kept thinking of Maine and how close it was to Canada. Spednic Lake bordered Canada and the US. Moosehead Lake was farther inland, but a boat could easily travel by water on Spednic to Canada, and the border patrol would be none the wiser.

Both men had relatively prominent positions at the time of the heist. He was well aware that a salary adequate for one man proved a mere pittance to another. Looking through his database, he saw that neither man seemed to be a spendthrift. Gambling could eat up a person's life savings in a heartbeat, though.

The next move was to search through their trash. Sifting through a person's trash was the quickest route to personal information. People threw away all kinds of secrets. Weekend garbage was the best, after a good cleaning spree. Clifton wondered if they put the garbage out the night before. Daytime was almost impossible. He could imagine the nosy neighbors calling the police and Bill having to come down to bail him out. He really hoped Cooper put his trash out the night before.

He'd make another trip to Wheeler's late that night.

The door to the outer office opened. He heard Olivia's voice, and promptly forgot about his jacket. He'd left her at her door again Sunday night. Being good had its drawbacks.

He went to meet her.

"Hi."

Olivia wore a purple pantsuit with a lavender blouse. Her gold necklace and earrings dazzled the eyes.

Clifton felt like a neighborhood Salvation Army customer by comparison.

He led her into his office.

"So what do we do today?" she asked.

He stopped in his tracks, raised an eyebrow. "We?"

"I might as well help out. I won't be a bit of good in the office."

"Olivia—"

"Don't Olivia me. I can scout out places just like

you can. I won't get in the way." She smiled, and that was Clifton's undoing. "I promise."

Still, he started to tell her to forget it, but on a personal level he'd love to spend the day with her. Besides, she'd get bored quickly after examining a few trash bags.

"Okay. I'm just going to check to see if Wheeler's trash is out today."

The day was beautiful. A soft wind blew, just cool enough so that it wasn't hot, but not enough to make it uncomfortable.

Monday wasn't trash day at Wheeler's townhouse.

"What do we do next?" Olivia asked.

"Stake out the place in the evenings and early mornings. Try to catch him dumping trash. Then I go through it." Luckily, his townhouse was fairly out of the way and couldn't be seen by too many other homes in the complex.

"You're almost like the paparazzi."

"Only we don't publish it for the world to see." What really troubled him was Joe, and why he was killed on that street corner late one night. He could very well have been the mastermind. The fact that the police and FBI had monitored Olivia's spending pattern so closely for the last few years was the only thing that eliminated her as a suspect. Of course, the fact that being around her, listening to her, and watching her expressions when she talked about the heist, he believed that she wasn't involved. But he couldn't detect those things in Joe. Joe wasn't around for him to read.

"The trash pickup day for Cooper in Chester Town is Thursday. They probably have two pickups each week, but I'm sure of that one. We'll skim through his trash late Wednesday night, if it's out."

"That's terrible. All kinds of germs are in trash." She scrunched up her nose.

"And information."

"I'll tag along to help out," she said quickly.

Clifton couldn't stifle a small laugh. Somehow he couldn't picture Olivia, wearing an elegant suit, turned up with her rear end in the air over a dirty garbage can. Wednesday night should prove interesting.

"Do you mind joining me for lunch at McDonald's?"

"McDonald's?"

"Sure. I eat there a lot."

"We aren't far from my house. I can whip up something better."

Clifton didn't have to deliberate. "You're on," he said, and headed to the beltway.

He drove through quiet neighborhoods to her townhouse, where she fixed a chef's salad piled high with lettuce, tomato, blanched broccoli, and cauliflower, and topped with grilled chicken, cheese, and crab meat, and served it with hot homemade rolls. When she'd first said what she was fixing, Clifton thought he'd have to ditch her after lunch so he could fill up at McDonald's, but the salad was filling and delicious.

"I'm sorry I don't have dessert. I don't keep it in the house, else I'll be tempted to eat it."

Clifton rubbed his stomach. "I couldn't eat another bite, but I still want my dessert."

He rose from his chair, rounded the table, and

pulled Olivia out of hers. Wrapping his arms around her, he leaned against the countertop and pulled her to him. Lowering his head, he kissed her long and hard. "Better than ice cream any day," he said, nibbling on her cheek.

Chapter 10

At the burst of dawn, as Monday night gave way to Tuesday, Clifton found himself parked a few cars down from Wheeler's townhouse. Moms and dads carried babies and dragged toddlers behind them to cold cars. Motors started, smoke streaming from the tailpipes as they pulled away. Some came with coffee in thermal mugs, steam trailing a path to the vehicles.

Clifton sipped his own coffee, leaned his head against the headrest, and continued his vigil. He had a long wait ahead of him.

Three hours later, Wheeler made an appearance. In one hand he carried a dark brown briefcase. With the other he dragged a trash can to the curb, depositing it in front of shrubbery and flowering bushes that were quickly losing their leaves.

Clifton slid lower in his seat so that he couldn't be seen when Wheeler went to his car. Wheeler started his BMW and waited a couple of minutes for the motor to warm before he pulled away from his parking spot. As soon as his car disappeared around the corner, Clifton started his motor and drove beside the trash area, surveying his surroundings as he opened the door. Another car started, idled for a minute, and drove away.

Clifton took the trash bag he'd stored in his passenger seat and held it in his hand as camouflage while he retrieved Wheeler's bag from the garbage can. Luckily, only one bag was inside. Taking a final glance around, he tossed both bags into his car trunk, which he'd lined earlier with plastic.

Gathering trash was always tricky during the day, he thought as he maneuvered through the rush hour traffic toward his house.

Once home, donning rubber gloves, he rummaged. Junk mail, remnants of bills, Maryland lottery tickets, garbage. Nothing incriminating.

He collected the trash, plastic lining, and gloves all into a huge black garbage bag and deposited it into the outside trash can.

He'd continue this same vigil for the next week until he found something—anything that would either exonerate Wheeler or condemn him.

He wouldn't see Olivia until later tonight. She'd gone into her office today to clear her schedule for the next few days. Otherwise, she'd be tagging along.

Clifton took another shower and dressed for work. So much of detective work was dead ends, but it was like fitting pieces to a puzzle. He gained enormous satisfaction when the pieces fit perfectly to make a complete picture.

* * *

On his way to the office Clifton dropped off several pairs of slacks and blazers at the cleaners. It was almost ten-thirty when he arrived.

"You got a message from Bobby Jones this morning," Veronica said.

"What did he say?"

"He wanted you to call him after four today. He left a number."

Clifton took the pink message sheet and carried it to his office. What could Jones want to talk to him about? Perhaps his brother had told him something, after all. It would be the break Clifton desperately needed.

He connected to the Internet and scanned his e-mail. Two messages were from his web service. Others were from professional links he was associated with.

He blinked twice and stopped at a message from Allen. His finger trembled on the keyboard at a mixture of hope and anticipation. He read the message—two short paragraphs—cherishing them as warmly as he would a two-page missive.

Allen thanked him for taking him to the game. He enjoyed Camden Yards, and hoped they could get together again. The Internet made talking easier than face-to-face confrontation.

After their talk Sunday night, Allen had loosened up just a little—not much, but Clifton was attuned to any small improvement. Although Allen hadn't initiated conversations, he hadn't dodged Clifton any longer, hadn't tried to get away as quickly as possible.

But the message meant so much more. Clifton took it as a signal that Allen was finally reaching out to him. He leaned back in his chair and smiled.

Clifton reflected on the easy camaraderie between Olivia and her children. Although she'd almost had to tie Craig down to keep him from taking over, there was that easy fluid acceptance, love and comfort between them. Craig had grown into a well-adjusted young man. Clifton wondered if it was the age difference or the relationship Olivia had developed with her children. Whatever it was, she'd done a fantastic job.

She must have had her hands full with him as a teenager. Craig definitely wanted to protect his mother. He wanted to stay in Maryland until it all was settled. But Olivia wouldn't hear of him missing classes. It wasn't his place to protect her, she'd told him. Olivia was the mother, and her edict was to be obeyed, even though her son was twenty. Needless to say, Craig and Rochelle were both on planes en route to their respective colleges Sunday afternoon.

Clifton scanned the remainder of his messages. There were notes from Craig and Rochelle, asking for updates on their mother. They wanted to make sure she wasn't holding anything back from them, and that she was safe. Clifton sighed. He'd better be prepared to e-mail them daily.

Someday he'd have that easy association with Allen.

He read his son's lines again, hoping that Allen was really saying that he enjoyed the time spent with his dad. Maybe his efforts were beginning to have some small results. Allen ended the message with the news that his mother was in town for a few days.

"Great."

"What was that?" Veronica called out.

"Nothing," Clifton said, stroking his chin. Perhaps it was time for him to close the chapter on his failed marriage. He and Catherine needed to talk. Clifton smirked. How he hated people who couldn't let the past end. He knew of couples who'd been divorced for ten years and couldn't stay in the same room together without hurling blasphemies across the room. He and Catherine didn't argue. They only exchanged money, from his hands to hers. Though he wasn't obligated to pay child support any longer, since Allen was eighteen, Clifton considered that he used his mother's home as his home base. He felt duty-bound to continue paying her something for his son's keep.

Clifton sighed. Maybe she needed the closure as much as he did. He wondered if she felt some measure of lingering unfinished business from their abrupt separation, despite the fact that she'd initiated it. Clifton wasn't above laying some blame at her door, even though he now accepted his share of the blunder. He hadn't been in that marriage alone, and neither had she.

Olivia went into the office earlier than usual on Tuesday morning. She organized her order for Cleopatra's Aromatherapy.

Olivia had lucked out four years ago at one of Cleo's open houses. Debra had heard about the shop from one of the parents whose children were in her daycare, and finagled an invitation for Olivia.

Olivia had been immediately impressed with the shop, and told Cleo about her spa. Cleo had given her jars of products to use in the hopes of gaining The Total Woman as a regular customer. The products she used were made with her own formulae.

Olivia and her employees had tried the merchandise on spa customers and themselves for facials and massages. Both her employees and the customers had loved the result, sending Olivia to the phone days later placing a large order and setting up an account for future business.

Now, Olivia even sold Cleo's line in her shop. Cleo had come over to set up the shelves in the reception area.

Olivia faxed an order of herbal massage creams and oils, gels, and scented face masks. She planned to spend the next week with Clifton without the worry of running out of products while she was away. With the extra duties heaped on Janice's shoulders while Olivia was away, she hated to place any more duties on her assistant.

"I thought you were on vacation," Janice said from the doorway.

"I'm trying to finish this so I can go in peace." Olivia glanced up from her desk.

"I'll believe it when it happens. You've been in almost every day since you mentioned you were going on vacation."

"I know. It's just—"

"The shop is your baby."

"Is it that bad?" Olivia put the order in a folder and handed it to Janice.

"It is."

"Well, I finally finished the papers you asked me to look through." She handed her another folder.

"Then there's no more to do." Janice clutched the two folders against her chest.

Olivia regarded her desk. "Actually the receptionist called in with a toothache. I'm going to fill in for her. Aren't you due at an accounting software seminar?"

Janice glanced at her watch. "I've got an hour to get there. The class is only ten minutes away." Janice rolled her eyes and shook her head. "You will never take a vacation from this place."

"I really am."

"I'll believe it when I see it." Disgusted, Janice disappeared from Olivia's door.

Olivia couldn't blame her. Hadn't she said a week ago that she was taking time off? And hadn't she been in the office almost every day since, if only for a little while?

Olivia left her office and headed to the reception area. In fifteen minutes the doors would open.

She opened the appointment book and placed it on the desk. The morning schedule would be very busy, she noticed, pleased. She recognized many of the names as nurses from P. G. Hospital. Sally was one of them.

The door opened. Olivia spoke to her employees as they filed in. She walked to the back room and turned a knob. Soft music mingled with a honeysuckle scent. One could barely smell it at all. Olivia believed in subtlety. Only a hint was necessary to create the pleasant ambiance she strove for.

Her first customer entered, looking harassed and tired. She'd worked the graveyard shift.

By noon, Olivia's spirits were in high gear. The cadence of the spa moved her, as did conversing with customers.

The spa was so much a part of her. It burst with life. It was her dream. Maybe that was what life was all about—to work at the place of your desire, but to have a life on the side, as well.

She was lucky that her employees were dependable. Truly, she knew her shop would run just fine without her. Her employees were that good, and she let them know with incentives and words how much she appreciated their commitment to The Total Woman.

She would take the time off and spend it on her own case with a clear conscience. More importantly, she'd spend the time with Clifton, not to mention speeding the investigation along. Perhaps she'd even shrink that twenty thousand.

At four Clifton called Olivia, telling her to pack a bag. They'd probably spend Wednesday night in Chester Town.

After that, he called Jones.

"I just remembered my brother was upset when the man got killed in a hit-and-run," Jones said. "I don't remember the name. I remember that Warren was real scared. He said something about how they got rid of that man because he knew too much."

Clifton's hand tightened on the phone. "What did he know?" he asked.

"Warren never said."

"Did he say who killed him?"

"Somebody with the company who planned the whole thing. He never gave me a name."

Clifton thanked him for the information and disconnected. He had a gut feeling that looking into Wheeler's and Cooper's affairs was the way to solve this case. They were very good at covering everything. And they had an enormous amount of patience.

Clifton drove to St. Mary's, where huge homes lay nestled on five-acre lots. Six cars were parked along the long driveway of the house in question. Clifton parked on the street under a huge weeping willow tree one house past the address Chandra had given him. It was the house where Wheeler gambled.

What did he see but Chandra's car parked two trees up on the other side? Clifton stifled an oath and opened his door. He walked to her car and all but pressed his face to her window.

She wasn't there. He wondered if she'd managed an invitation to join the group. Chandra didn't have the money for a high-stakes game. Clifton hiked in the direction of the house, keeping close to huge shrubbery and trees. He almost walked up on Chandra before he saw her, wearing brown jeans and a sweatshirt, watching the group within through cheap binoculars.

"What the hell are you doing here?" he demanded, his voice low.

Startled, she muffled a shriek, stepped back, then clutched a hand to her chest when she recognized him.

"It's obvious, isn't it? I'm following Wheeler. There's loads of chips on that table."

"I want you to leave and forget about following Wheeler," he whispered. "You're biting off more than you can chew."

"I've—"

"Use your time to find a job. Leave the rest to us."

"There's the reward."

"Don't worry. If there's a reward you'll get your share."

She turned stubborn. "I've got just as much a right to be here as you do."

A dog barked from a distance. They fell silent until the barking stopped.

"You're walking a thin line as it is. Don't start with your rights," Clifton continued.

She tried another tactic. "If it wasn't for me you wouldn't even know about this place."

"Yeah, but I do know." He turned her in the direction of her car. "Go home."

She sighed and started plodding toward her car, dragging her feet. Clifton followed her. She inserted her key and opened the door.

"Chandra, this is more than you can handle. I want you to stay away from this. I regret now not having you arrested. At least then you'd be safe. Out here messing with this heist isn't safe. Leave it to people who know what they're doing."

She nodded.

Clifton only wished he could believe her as he watched her start her motor and drive away.

He got his camera and binoculars out of his car and returned to the spot they'd just vacated—behind a high lavender bush with just enough branches to hide behind. With the lights shining out back, he didn't want to chance being seen. A backdrop of trees and a flower garden separated him from the forest. He could lie in wait for hours undetected.

He peered through high-powered binoculars. The family room window was high, and without window treatment.

The game was going fast and furious. Chips passed hands quickly. Cigar smoke filled the air, forming a cloudy residue that mingled with cigarette smoke. Shot glasses of Kentucky bourbon had created a lively but serious bunch.

Clifton wasn't fooled by the jeans and sweatsuits, as he snapped pictures. Judging from the Cadillacs, Mercedes, and BMW's in the driveway, it was a well-heeled group of high rollers who leaned their heads back in laughter, frowned in concentration and worry, and smiled when they dragged a colossal stack of chips near them.

At around 2:00 A.M., Clifton saw huge stacks of bills—hundreds and twenties—appear on the table. Wheeler's stash was just as lucrative as the others. Bills soon replaced the chips in each pile. Wheeler seemed to have lost a great deal, judging from the lack of chips in front of him and by the piles of money slipping from him to the others. This definitely wasn't a nickel-and-dime game.

Where did the extra money come from? Clifton wondered. Wheeler had distinctly said that he no longer gambled. He attended regular meetings at Gambler's Anonymous. Fat lot of good that did him.

Clifton made his way back to his car as the men

filed out of the huge house. Slinging his camera and
binoculars on the seat, he slumped low, waiting for
the cars to pass. Wheeler's car was the last to leave.
Clifton started his motor and fell in at a discreet
distance behind the maroon BMW.

He rubbed his eyes and poured cold coffee into a
cup. He needed the caffeine kick to keep him awake
on the drive home.

What seemed like an eternity later, Wheeler parked
in front of his townhouse. Clifton debated whether
to approach him, but decided to leave that for tomorrow.

At four-thirty Wednesday afternoon, Clifton leaned
against his car in front of Wheeler's townhouse,
watching the man pull into the slot beside Clifton's
Taurus.

"Hello," the man said. "Zayne, was it?" He extended
a hand.

Clifton nodded, returned his handshake.

"What can I do for you?" He glanced around as a
neighbor came out with a toddler. "Why don't we
go inside?"

Clifton followed him. The interior was decorated
tastefully and with a masculine edge. An emerald-
burgundy-and-gold striped sofa in the living room
was flanked by cherry wood tables. Wheeler motioned
him to a seat.

"So what brings you here this time?"

"During our last conversation you mentioned that
you were involved with Gamblers Anonymous. However, you were seen at a poker game last night."

Wheeler blew out a long breath.

"A game where you lost lots of money."

Wheeler got up and paced to the fireplace mantel. "I stopped going to meetings a month ago."

"Did you use the money from the heist to pay for your losses?"

"Hell, no. I've told you before I had nothing to do with that heist." He sat on a plush chair, planted his elbows on his knees, and scrubbed a hand over his face.

"Well, where did the money come from?"

"I won a hundred grand in the Maryland lottery." Leaving his seat, he went to a tiny desk in the corner, pulled out a drawer, and brought the check stub to Clifton. He really had won the money.

After a few more questions, Clifton thanked him for the information and left. The check didn't exonerate him, but Clifton could use a break someplace. So far, it didn't lead to Wheeler.

Chapter 11

At ten-thirty Wednesday night, Clifton and Olivia parked outside Cooper's house, across the street by the park. Half the street was lined with trash cans, but the designated space at the Cooper's curb was empty. The light still shining inside the house offered hope that someone would bring it out before the night was over.

The neighborhood was quiet, and most had settled down for the night. A man two doors to the left walked a collie to the park, near where Clifton had parked half an hour ago. The man didn't give the car a second glance.

Tonight, Clifton drove Bill's BMW with its tinted windows. A BMW blended in perfectly in that neighborhood. Besides, it wouldn't do to have Cooper recognize Clifton's Taurus.

He could see perfectly well through the windows,

but under the cover of night, outsiders couldn't see in.

A pizza delivery car careened to a stop in front of a house down the street. The driver hopped out and all but ran to the door with the heat-protecting package. *Must be on the thirty-minute time restriction,* thought Clifton.

A car with loud rock blaring on the radio pulled into the driveway three houses up. Two teenagers exited and disappeared inside the house. Five minutes later, three boys strolled to the car, laughing. Three doors shut, and the car pulled off.

Just a normal suburban community, Clifton thought as he reached for his cooling coffee. The neighborhood had a pulse of its own.

"This is one busy neighborhood for so late at night," Olivia remarked, uncapping the thermos to top his cup. "You'd think children would be in bed on a school night."

"Probably seniors, stretching their wings."

"Uh-huh."

Clifton tried to forget about the subtle scent of the perfume she wore, the tight jeans and V-neck top that displayed a hint of breast. It took enormous control not to reach over and haul her into his arms. Only the knowledge that Cooper could arrive while he was necking in the front seat suppressed his actions.

A light from an approaching vehicle blazed down the street. He and Olivia tensed when, for a second, the headlights flashed in the car. The garage door opened electronically at Cooper's house just before his white Mercedes pulled into the driveway. He drove into the slot, and the door closed. Clifton got a peek at him, wearing a dark blue suit, just before the door closed.

Grabbing the binoculars from the middle of the seat, he looked into what appeared to be the den. It faced the street, and was located to the right of the door. Cooper and his wife entered but didn't bother to close the blinds that were thrown partially open, offering Clifton and Olivia an unimpaired view.

Cooper had already discarded his jacket and tie. He put his briefcase on the floor and sat behind a mahogany desk on an emerald-green, cushioned seat.

His wife stood angrily in front of the desk. She threw a letter at him. It perched near the edge closest to him. Cooper opened it and read the contents. He placed it on the desk and spoke calmly to his wife. She threw up her hands and continued to rant, pacing back and forth in front of the window, finally wagging a finger at him.

If only Clifton were a fly on the wall and could listen in.

"What's going on in there?" Olivia asked, twisting in her seat. "You don't think that Chandra is trying to blackmail him, too, do you?"

"I should hope not. They wouldn't let her off as easily as you did." The thought nagged him, especially after seeing her last night at the poker game. The silly girl could very well have disregarded his warning. Fear seemed foreign to her. Even a little fear would keep her safer.

"Especially if he's the one we're looking for."

"If he is, she could end up in more trouble than she could handle. People have killed for a lot less than twenty mil." He sincerely hoped she'd heeded his advice. "Maybe we should have reported her."

"I couldn't do that. I don't want her to become another one lost in the system. It's such a mess. And it only gets worse once they get tangled up in it."

She thought just like the mother she was, Clifton thought, always thinking of what was best for the children. In this case, he wondered if Chandra would stay safe. She could be her own worst enemy.

Finally, Cooper stood and walked around the desk. He pulled his wife toward him and held her by her arms. She knocked his hands away and walked away quickly.

Clifton snorted. With all the drama, he might as well be watching a daytime soap. He glanced at his watch. It flashed ten forty-five. He settled deeper into the cushions, and waited. Surely someone would bring out the trash soon.

"Coffee?" Olivia held up the thermos again.

"Thanks," he said just to give her something to do.

"Is it always like this? You sit and wait, and sit and wait?"

"Most times. It's boring stuff, isn't it?"

Cooper went to the safe and opened it. He took something out.

Clifton adjusted his binoculars, straining to identify the object. It was money. The man sat at his desk and counted small bills. Clifton leaned forward, trying to get a look in the safe, but Cooper's body blocked it.

"Definitely not what I imagined." She handed him a Styrofoam cup. "Sandwich?"

"Sure," Clifton replied absentmindedly.

"I packed turkey and ham."

"Turkey."

She rattled around in a paper bag and put the sandwich on the dash in front of him.

"What are you looking at?"

"He's counting money."

"Oh, my God! Chandra's blackmailing him."

"Let's not rush to conclusions. There could be some other reason. People do sometimes keep money in their safes." But Clifton believed the money was for Chandra. *Damn. How could she be so stupid?*

"We've got to stop her."

"We'll call her from the hotel."

Finally Cooper closed the safe. He put a rubber band around the money and stuffed it into his briefcase. He sat at his desk again and shuffled through papers.

After ten minutes, Clifton put the binoculars down and reached for his sandwich. Opening the wrapper, he pulled it out and bit into turkey, cheese, tomato, lettuce, mayo, and mustard. Olivia had fixed it exactly the way he loved them.

Half an hour passed and Cooper sat at the computer, now typing away.

Someone passed, walking a German shepherd.

"I bet you wish you'd stayed at home by now," Clifton said.

"This is interesting." She didn't eat, only drank the coffee. "Gives me a feel for what you do."

To Olivia it was warm and cozy in the car. Any time spent with Clifton was better than at home and alone, though she didn't have a problem with her own company. If *she* were here alone, she'd be bored stiff.

* * *

At midnight, the light was still on in the Cooper household, but the trash wasn't on the street yet. They'd had to wipe the condensation from the windows several times.

Olivia had had to go to the bathroom for the last half hour. Now, she felt she could almost float away.

Cooper was on the phone. As he talked, he held the letter his wife had thrown to him.

"Clifton, I need to go to the ladies' room." He had the binoculars trained on the den, but he took one hand, reached under the seat, and pulled out a bottle. Absentmindedly, he handed it to her. He went back to his perusal of the den.

Olivia held the bottle with its secure, wide-capped screw top away from her and eased it onto the floor under Clifton's legs. Reaching into her purse she took out her antibiotic hand gel and poured some into her hands. Maybe she could wait a little while longer without floating away, she thought as she rubbed the solution into her hands. But five minutes later, the situation had worsened. She shouldn't have drunk all that coffee.

"Ah, Clifton." She cleared her throat. "What am I supposed to do with that bottle?" she asked in the quiet interior.

He glanced at her as if he'd forgotten she was there.

Clifton swiped a hand across his head. "I guess the bottle won't work. He's not going to put the trash out tonight. We might as well leave."

All the gas stations they'd passed were closed. The town looked closed up for the night. He drove to a

hotel ten miles down the road with the vacancy sign
flashing.

"We'll get a hotel room now, and see if we can
check the garbage early in the morning. Maybe even
walk along the beach before we leave."

"Fine, as long as I can get to a rest room."

Clifton checked into a room with two double beds,
hoping they'd only use one.

Olivia sailed into the bathroom and used the facili-
ties, thankful she wasn't an investigator. She washed
her hands and opened the door.

Clifton had brought in her purse, the bag with
sandwiches and drinks, and a duffel bag.

"How do you sit for hours that way?" she asked.

"The glass bottle works for me. There's a major
difference between us."

"I'll say." Olivia sat on the edge of the bed.

"But I like the difference." He raised his eyebrows
suggestively and, enjoying the pleasure of Olivia's
face, he removed his notebook from his pocket. He
sat on the edge of the bed and flipped the pages to
where he'd recorded Chandra's number. Picking up
the phone, he dialed.

Chandra answered sleepily after the fourth ring.
"Yeah?" she barked.

"This is Clifton Zayne."

Silence was followed by, "Do you know what time
it is?"

"I'll do the questioning. Have you blackmailed anyone else?"

"No."

"Don't lie to me."

"I haven't. I even have a job at Finger Lickin' Fried

Chicken. I start tomorrow, and you're cutting into my sleep."

"These people have murdered before. They won't hesitate to get rid of you, especially if you blackmail the wrong one."

"Look, I'm not stupid. I blackmailed Olivia because I knew she was safe."

"I hope you're being straight with me," Clifton said.

"If you don't believe me, call the place tomorrow. I'll be there."

"You can count on it."

Chandra dropped the phone on the cradle. She blew out a huge breath and ran a shaky hand through her tousled hair. There was no way Ray and Harvey had discussed the blackmail with him, or knew who she was.

Olivia and Clifton were full of shit if they thought she was going to work in some minimum wage, fast-food joint and let that cretin go free.

Chandra was just going to work there long enough to get Miss Goody Two-shoes Olivia off her back, and then she'd quit—with ten grand stashed under her mattress—five from Ray, and five from Harvey. That'd keep her going until she could prove Ray was the blackmailer. Her dad had known Ray. Ray could have talked him into committing the robbery. And Ray was living in that nice townhouse while she stayed in this roach-infested, one-bedroom hovel.

Chandra plumped up her pillow and snuggled under the covers. She had a long day ahead of her.

* * *

"What did Chandra say?" Olivia asked.

"She has a new job at some fast-food chicken place."

"Thank God," Olivia murmured, opening her suitcase.

"Yeah." Clifton hoped she'd been straight with him. He had his reservations.

Clifton stood. "While you get comfortable, I'm going to make another trip out there."

"I'll go with you."

He collected his keys from the dresser. "Let's go, then."

By the time they reached Cooper's the trash can was on the curb and the house was dark. The breeze coming off the Chesapeake Bay was brisk, cool, soothing. And the street had finally quieted.

Clifton reached for the door handle, but the knocking coming from a trash can stopped him. He picked up his binoculars, twisted in his seat, and focused. A raccoon explored the base of a garbage can farther up the street. He made such a racket that Clifton wondered why someone hadn't come out to investigate.

They waited, waited, and waited more, until the raccoon traveled to another street and everything quieted once again. It was 2:00 A.M. when Clifton disengaged the interior light so it wouldn't shine when he climbed out of the car. Taking the penlight from the glove compartment, he opened his door. Easing it closed, he crossed the street.

Olivia watched on anxiously for about three minutes before she grabbed a plastic bag out of the backseat and shook out of the contents. Grabbing it in her arm, she opened her door, easing it shut just as Clifton had. Two people were much faster than one, she reasoned as she crossed the street.

"What?" Clifton jumped back when he saw the dog at her feet.

"Shh. It's a stuffed collie. I'm going to help you."

He let loose a low curse. "Here, hold the light so I can see." He put the penlight in her hand. She pointed it into the trash can as he carefully sorted through the mess. Picking up the leash, she angled the stuffed dog on the sidewalk. If they got caught, at least walking the dog was a legitimate excuse for being on the street at 2:00 A.M.

"Hold up the bag I left on the ground."

Olivia glanced around, but didn't see a bag. "Where?" she asked.

"There." He looked to the left. "Check my pocket."

Olivia dug into his pockets, felt his muscled thigh—that kicked her heart into high gear—before her fingers slid against the plastic. Pulling out the bag, she held it open for him, glancing around.

Clifton sorted through old food, bones, used paper towels, an old toothbrush, dog hair, paper wrappers, meat cartons, a woman's razor. Discarding them all, he rammed handwritten and typed papers, bills, and notes into the bag.

They heard a door squeak open. Clifton quickly closed the lid to the can, snatched the dog out of Olivia's hand, and led her across the street to the park and set the dog on the ground. They moved deeper into the trees.

They heard a car start up and drive away.

"I've gone through everything. Let's go," he said, leading her back to the car.

Olivia took her pet in her arms, and they walked slowly to the opening.

Clifton peeled off the gloves, throwing them into the garbage bag.

Once they were on their way to the hotel, Olivia burst into laughter, catching a stitch in her side.

Clifton joined her. "You brought a stuffed dog? Lady, you've got quite an imagination."

"Whatever works." The adrenaline flowed high on their drive. In minutes, they were in the hotel with the trash he'd collected spread out on the table— remnants of the electric bill, cable bill, a note their daughter wrote to a friend and discarded, a grocery list, an envelope with a Canadian return address, six credit card offers, old newspapers, a book club offer, CD club offers, soccer camp brochures.

Inside a manila envelope they found an envelope with the return address to an offshore bank. Clifton discarded everything except the envelopes with the Canadian and offshore addresses. The window envelope didn't show the name that had been used on the account.

"So what does this all mean?" Olivia asked.

"The offshore bank account means he's probably hiding money. But he's not using it here. We need to know who's at this Canadian address."

"How will you do that?" Olivia asked, rubbing eyes gritty with fatigue. She opened her suitcase and pulled out nightclothes.

"I don't pay for Canadian databases because we

don't get enough business there. We have a contact there I'll call tomorrow."

Olivia blew out a huge breath. It was amazing how exhausted a person could get from just sitting around. Everything was so tedious in this business. She'd had no idea.

"I'm taking a shower." She gathered her night-clothes and a toiletries bag and sauntered to the bath-room.

Clifton entered the bathroom right after Olivia fin-ished. Her very feminine scented bath gel hit him like a brick wall, and traveled straight below his belt. "Just great," he thought, his body reacting to the fragrance.

"Did you say something?" Olivia called out.

"Uh, no." He was as hard as a brick. He shucked his clothing and turned on the water, twisting the nozzle to cool, lest he'd frighten her. She'd led pretty much a sheltered life the last few years. Climbing into the shower, he used the hotel soap, which wasn't too bad.

Clifton climbed into bed after his shower. Olivia went back into the rest room. It sounded as if she were washing out something. Then she returned to her bed, her scent circling in the air. He really tried to be good, but he couldn't sleep after she got into bed.

This was supposed to be innocent, but hell, he was just a man, not a saint.

"Olivia?"

She cleared her throat. "Yes?"

"Are you sleepy?" Great. He sounded like a teen-ager. Allen could come up with a better line. But he wasn't exactly thinking with his brain right now.

"Can't sleep a wink." She rolled on her side to face him, the covers rolling off her shoulders.

He observed her closely. The outside light leaked in from around the curtain edges.

The springs of his mattress grumbled as he shifted his weight. He propped his head up with his elbow. "Five years ago, when my wife left me and took away my son, I swore I'd never love a woman or care for one as I'd cared for her."

"Oh, no."

"And the women I've dated since have all been the type who is only interested in the moment. I purposely dated women who weren't looking for permanence. And then I got tired of that game. I was just another lay among many."

"Not to mention safety."

"I always—always—use protection. And I take tests and require the same from them—before."

The room grew quiet for moments. "Sounds pretty clinical," she finally said.

"The relationships were meaningless."

"I could never do that."

He already knew that. "And then I met you. You are a woman before her time. My parents were loyal to each other. They weren't demonstrative, but they looked out for each other. But you . . . " He weighed his words. "When all the chips were stacked against your husband, you still believed in him because of the special bond you shared. Do you realize how rare that is today? Some women would have thought that he'd let them down, leaving them without the protection of insurance to raise two children alone."

"I couldn't blame him. We both grew up poor. We were both naive. I was as responsible as he. We just did the best we knew how at the time."

"But you still believed him—you still loved him." A wistful sigh escaped.

The bed rustled as he shifted the covers back, swung his legs over the side and crossed the aisle to her. He sat on the edge of Olivia's bed and searched for her hands, taking them in his warm embrace.

Her honeyed voice was heady.

"When I asked to take you out, I didn't expect to fall for you. And this isn't just to get you into bed with me. You've brought me back to life. You've made me believe in what I thought I could never have. I know this sounds corny, but I feel like an iceberg coming to life. And I don't want to make the same mistakes with you."

He released one of her hands and outlined her face. Olivia turned her mouth to his hand.

He inhaled sharply. "There's an indescribable joy in knowing there's someone close you connect with." His voice was hoarse.

Olivia took her free hand and caressed him. "You know, since Joe died I've never expected to find love again. I'm not a saint. I've had a couple of brief relations since—very brief, and years ago." Clifton shifted positions, reclined beside Olivia, letting her head rest on his shoulder, his left arm around her waist. "But we never connected, and it was too emotionally destructive. I had two children to rear, and they were my priority. Part of my reticence is the fact that I'm overweight." She inhaled sharply when he bought his hand to her waist. "I'm not the kind of woman men look at and want to sleep with. Men like thin, well-toned women."

"Not all men."

"Most do. They want women who resemble those slender models in magazines, or gorgeous actresses on television. And I have to say that I've tried." She laughed, a self-deprecating hollow laugh. "Lord, did I try. Every diet that came along, I tried. I would lose, then gain, lose and gain again. It's been a vicious cycle. Until I promised myself that I wasn't going to diet again. Ever.

"Then my daughter asked me to start walking with her, and I did. I'd do anything for my children. And I enjoyed it with the two of them. I think I've lost twenty pounds over the last year, but I've got plenty more to go. I don't know if I'll ever lose that thirty pounds. But I know the walking is a health benefit, so I'll continue."

"A man who looks only at your weight doesn't deserve your gentleness or your goodness. Olivia, when I met you, you stole my heart." He nuzzled her forehead, wanting to absorb her pain, wanting to impart her worth. Her value was more than her size— so much more. "Besides, I like a woman with meat on her bones. I think I'm man enough to handle you—all of you."

"Are you sure about that?"

His hands stilled, his breath was a hiss. "Do you want to go there?"

She paused, glancing up at him in the darkness. "Yes," she whispered, her soft breath brushing his face.

"Olivia . . ." His hands ran up and down her arms. "It's been a long time for you. Are you sure you're ready?"

"I'm ready."

"First, preliminaries. I don't have any diseases. And I test once a year. I want to get that straight up front."

"Neither do I."

"But I do have protection."

"I like a man who comes prepared." Her soft words whispered against his neck.

Tilting her chin, he lowered his head, pressed his lips to hers. Smoothing his hand down her side, he crushed her softness against him and almost exploded.

"I'm trying to take this slow and easy," he croaked against her lips and settled his mouth over hers, pressing firmly and opening, edging his tongue inside to mingle with hers.

Olivia could only groan, enjoy, and let her tongue dance with his. He shifted, bringing his hips firmly against hers, the thin silk separating them, no protection against his hardness, his warmth. Excitement started in her middle and blossomed out.

"Do you like that, honey?" His warm breath mingled with hers.

"Yes," she whispered, reaching up to touch him.

With an exquisite touch his hands stroked her hips, slid inside her panties, taking his sweet time, letting her enjoy his caress thoroughly before he shifted to slide up to her abdomen.

Ending the kiss, he slid his hard body down hers,

loving the contrast of softness and strength. He unhooked her silk bra and caught one nipple in his mouth, swirling his tongue over her, kneading the other with his hand. His unhurried, exquisite movements took Olivia's breath away. It was as if he intended to take the rest of the night with her.

Olivia's heart pounded against her chest as he moved from one area to another. She let her hands learn the pulse and texture of his body.

She'd forgotten how extraordinary it was to touch a man—how much pleasure she derived from a caress.

Their ritual dance continued until finally they came together as one, moving as one. The ultimate explosion snatched her breath away, stealing his heart.

After their heartbeats slowed to a natural pulse, Olivia slept peacefully in Clifton's arms.

Despite their lack of sleep, Clifton and Olivia dressed in jeans and sweatshirts with sneakers early the next morning. He drove to the beach. The wind was brisk, and the temperature was cool as they donned lightweight jackets.

They walked, using a brisk pace along the hard sand-packed shore. They had the beach to themselves, except for just the seagulls. Olivia stopped to pick up shells along the trek. A playful hour spent talking, chasing, and playing left them lighthearted and hungry.

Clifton didn't jog as he usually did, but kept his pace with Olivia. When it was all over, they reluctantly returned to the real world.

* * *

Three hours later, Clifton was back at his office. He called the offshore bank, pretending to be Cooper. No accounts were listed under that name.

Realizing that he'd be going to Maine soon, he checked the database for the day of his flight, the airline he used, and the time of arrival.

Cooper was leaving early Saturday morning, which meant that Clifton had to arrive in Maine no later than Friday morning to drive to Canada to check out the address on the envelope in Frederickton.

Before he left, he hoped to have the name of the person living at that address from his Canadian contact.

Clifton glanced at his watch. It was two-thirty.

"Veronica?"

"Yes?"

"Make me reservations to Bangor, Maine, for tomorrow morning, please."

"When will you return?"

"I don't know yet. Say three days for the ticket, and I'll pay the penalty if I change it." He dialed Olivia's number. When she picked up, he told her about the Maine trip and she insisted on traveling with him.

He had Veronica book two seats.

At six, Clifton was seated in a Baltimore restaurant near Morgan State, with his ex-wife. He waited until they finished their meal and lingered over coffee

before he asked her what he should have asked her
five years ago. "Why did you leave?"

She silently stirred a spoonful of sugar in her coffee
while he waited for her response. "You know, Cliff,
back then I thought that if I put distance between us
you would suddenly see that I meant so much to you,
that you couldn't help but come after us. I was so
lonely at home, and nothing I did would move you
to spend time with Allen and me." She gazed at her
hands and then at him. "More than the money and
trappings, I needed *you*."

"Then why didn't you say so?"

"I did. Every time I suggested we go out. The movies. A drive to the park. The mountains. Anything.
Something." She looked down again and cleared her
throat. "And then once I moved, I started to go out
with Blair. It was innocent and casual at first. I was
new in town. He was a single father with a son Allen's
age. We started just doing things with the kids. But
in the process we became close."

Clifton tightened his lips in anger. He'd been faith-
ful to her. Never once had it crossed his mind to go
out with another woman, no matter how attractive
she was—how lonely he was. Why should it have been
different for her? "Lady, going out with another man
is never casual. You opened the door to destroying
our marriage."

"Destroy what? We were two people who shared a
house. Little more."

"We shared a son, too."

She inhaled sharply. "You seem to need to know
why it happened, and I'm trying to tell you. I know
it was my fault. Blair and I just did simple things

like walk in the park. He came to Allen's games. Sometimes we went boating together, explored museums together. You never came, and I knew I couldn't settle for what we had any longer. I wasn't willing to have an affair with another man while I was still married to you. The only option left was a divorce. I know it all seems vain, because you did provide for us. But I wanted more. I wanted you. I didn't want to have to look elsewhere for what I should have had with my husband."

"I wish . . . " Clifton didn't know what to say past the hurt and lingering anger clinging to his gut.

"This is harder than I thought it would be. I asked you a thousand times to take us places. To just carve out a little time for us. And then I'd feel guilty because you did work so hard. I thought that I shouldn't expect anything more. I mean, with women suffering with husbands on drugs, abusive husbands, alcoholic husbands, husbands who won't work, what right did I have to complain when you did nothing but work and provide for us? I started to feel that my needs were silly in comparison. But I couldn't live the way things were any longer. The decision I made was the most difficult one in my life."

"Catherine, I always wanted to care for you. I wanted you to have the best. Remember when you said in elementary school you wore shoes and socks with holes in them, and the kids teased you? I didn't want you and Allen to go through that, to feel less than anyone else because I couldn't provide enough. I wanted you to hold your heads up high with pride."

She shook her head. "I'm sorry—so sorry, Clifton. I know you gave me so much, all the material things

I ever wanted and more. But I didn't have you." She glanced across the room and back at him. "I guess we should have had this talk five years ago."

He took her hand in his. "Are you happy now?"

She nodded. "I'm very happy. I just hope you've found some happiness, too."

Clifton thought of Olivia, and his heart swelled. Her life had been as hard as his. She understood his drive because she had a family to provide for on her own. They were very suited to each other. "I have."

As he drove back to his apartment, Clifton was glad he'd finally talked with Catherine. It was time to let his anger go and begin anew with Allen and Olivia. Thank God she had come to him at this time in his life, when he was ready for a serious relationship. He wondered if he could have appreciated her a year ago, or even six months ago. He did know that he'd grown tired of meaningless affairs.

Olivia was a special woman, and he only wanted the best for her. This time the best was the closeness they shared. First he needed to solve her case, and then he'd see where the future carried them.

He frowned. He wondered if he'd make the same mistakes all over again with Olivia that he'd made in his first marriage. He was starting a new business that required an enormous amount of time. Sometimes he wouldn't be able to spend time with Olivia, regardless of how much he wanted to. Would he find himself neglecting her the way he neglected Allen and his mother?

He hoped not. But then he realized that part of the solution was awareness, and now that he was aware he'd work hard not to make the mistakes he'd made before.

Debra wiped away the tears streaming from her eyes.

"And when I had to pee so much I was crossing my legs, he hands me a bottle. A glass bottle! Can you believe that?" Olivia asked her.

Debra howled with laughter, bending over, stretching out, and doubling up again. "And you want to go with him to Maine?"

"It doesn't get boring."

"Girl, you have lost your mind," Debra said, untangling her legs and moving them to a more comfortable position. Taking a tissue from the holder, she dabbed at her eyes.

Olivia had spread a picnic on the cocktail table in the middle of the family room floor. She and Debra sat on huge pillows. They liked to do this about once every six months. Ladies' Night Out, they called it.

"You're going as far north as you can get, out in the middle of nowhere, to investigate a murder and robbery? We've tried some wild and innovative things in our day, but that's stretching things, even for you."

"I won't be alone. Clifton will be with me." A secret smile tugged at her lips.

"You just met the man."

"But it feels as if I've known him forever."

Debra only shook her head at Olivia's craziness. "When you come out, you really come out, don't you?"

Olivia sipped her wine. "Do you remember when

Craig and Rochelle first went to camp? Tonya and her children spent the night at her mother's house?"

Debra nodded. "We were so tired that night. It was ten, and we wanted to celebrate having the place to ourselves."

"And we spread this old quilt on the living room floor."

"The only crackers we had were saltines."

"That peanut butter on saltines was a delicacy."

They laughed and glanced at the table. Today they had meatballs with a barbecue sauce, artichoke hearts, shrimp cocktail, fresh strawberries, blackberries, and kiwi with a vanilla yogurt sauce, and spiced Russian tea.

"We've come a long way, baby," Debra said.

"We certainly have."

"I hope you know what you're doing."

"When have I ever known what I was doing? We always go by the seat of our pants."

"We're too old for that." She chuckled. "Just be safe, Olivia. You're like a sister to me."

"Oh, Debra. I feel more alive with Clifton than I've felt in years." She crossed her arms under her breasts, rubbed her arms with her hands, and sighed. "Even if I don't know what I'm getting into, he knows."

"Olivia . . ."

"Yes?"

"You are glowing. He's absolutely perfect for you."

"I know I've lost my mind, just like you said. Because I'm in love with him."

"I know," Debra said wistfully. "You don't know how to have a casual affair. It's all or nothing."

Chapter 12

Clifton and Olivia disembarked in Bangor, Maine, the next morning and rented a car at the airport. Their first stop was a large grocery store. They purchased sandwich fixings, cereal, snacks, fruit, sodas, milk, and juice, and packed it all in a Styrofoam cooler. Food wasn't always readily available on stakeouts.

Clifton snatched a bag of tortilla chips and a container of salsa off the shelf.

"Do we need to make any more stops?"

Olivia arranged the cold storage items in the ice in the cooler. She thrust an empty bag into his hand. "A fast-food place for coffee," she said.

He glanced around. "There's one across the street."

They piled into the car. In a couple of minutes they

parked in one of many open slots. "We'd better make a pit stop while we're at it," Clifton said.

After that first night of discomfort, Olivia hardly needed reminding.

First using the rest room, Olivia filled their thermos with hot coffee and bought two cups to drink then. They'd drink the coffee in the thermos later. Shutting the door, they started on their journey.

Traveling east, they drove through Vanceboro, a border town where Cooper's cabin was located on Spednic Lake. Locating it would have to wait until they returned from Canada.

Just before they left for the airport, the PI they'd contacted in Canada told them a Mary Hooper lived at the address on the envelope.

Clifton was well aware that people often chose names close to their actual name when using aliases.

They drove on Route 6 to the Canada/Maine border crossing. Only a few minutes were spent at the border station, where they answered a few questions. They were tourists spending a day in Frederickton, visiting museums. They were allowed passage into New Brunswick.

From this point they took the scenic drive—bordered with several species of pine trees and elm—on roads that curved around the hills.

Armed with an AAA map, they discovered that Mary Hooper's house was situated in an older development near the Saint John River. The two-story structure had a patch of green grass in the front yard, but the flowers were long gone. Winter came early in those parts, and the leaves had turned to gorgeous, more vibrant hues than back in Maryland, where the days were still long and the temperature mild.

They watched a woman they presumed to be Mary come out the house, get in her car, and leave.

Clifton snapped pictures.

An older woman next door lugged a suitcase into her car trunk and disappeared back inside her own house.

"I'm going to talk to her." Clifton shrugged into his jacket.

Olivia put a hand on his arm. "Let me," she said. "She'll be more open with another woman."

"Hurry up, then, before Mary Hooper returns."

Olivia hurried into her coat, opened the door to a cold wind that snatched her breath away. And it was only October. Tightening her coat around her, she rushed to Hooper's door and pressed the doorbell, the wind whipping at her legs. She wished she'd remembered her hat. When no one answered, she rapped her knuckles against the wooden surface, waiting for the woman next door to reappear.

"She's gone for the day," said the woman, who wore a dark brown skirt with matching pumps. A short winter jacket protected her from the cold, but the wind didn't seem to bother her as it did Olivia. She carried another suitcase.

"Oh, no." Olivia put on the best crestfallen face that she could muster. She glanced at her watch. "I'm only in town for a few hours. I'd hoped to see her while I'm here," she said, biting her bottom lip in distress.

"You're from the States."

"Yes, from Philly." Then she remembered where she was. "That's Philadelphia, Pennsylvania."

The woman smiled. "I've heard of it." Nodding, she dropped the suitcase on the ground. "Never been there, though. Don't know how long Mary will be gone. Her husband's coming into town tomorrow. Who are you?"

"I know a friend of hers. She asked me to stop by while I'm here."

"If you can stick around a while, you'll see her later on, I guess."

"Afraid I can't do that." Olivia sighed regretfully. "I'll be on my way back by then."

"That's too bad. You're going to miss little Alice." The woman smiled. Crow's-feet crinkled at the corners of her lively eyes. "They're going to take her out of the Mountain Magic home for a little vacation. She loves that."

"The home?" Olivia frowned.

"She's got liver problems, you know. They say she may be able to come home for good in a few months. She's gotten a lot better."

"That's wonderful!"

"It's amazing what doctors can do. They actually did a procedure where she grew a new liver."

"Amazing," Olivia said. Olivia glanced down the street. "This is such a wonderful neighborhood for children."

The woman nodded. "It is. I miss my little one. Both my girls grew up here."

"How old is Alice now?"

"Fourteen, I think. She's been at the Mayo Clinic down in the States, and it's *very* expensive. She had some complications, and had to stay at a clinic here for a while.'' She nodded her head, dragging out the words. ''The little girl is why Mary can't travel with her husband. She likes to be near her daughter.''

''I would imagine so.''

''But I tell her, now that Alice is better, a vacation with her husband won't hurt. He needs your time, too,'' she whispered. ''He must be a rich one.''

''What *is* his name?'' Olivia tapped her finger against her mouth. ''My friend mentioned it. Harvey?''

''Harry. He's the nicest man. Always a sweet disposition. Mary's so lucky to have him.''

''She is. Well, I won't hold you. It's nice meeting you. I hope you enjoy your trip.''

''I'm going to visit my daughter.'' The woman bent and picked up her suitcase. ''Her first baby is due any day now.''

''Congratulations!''

Olivia returned to the car and relayed the information to Clifton. ''Could you start the car, please? It's freezing out there.''

He started the motor, turning the heat up full blast.

''So all those fishing trips were actually trips to Canada,'' he said, regarding her, a minute later.

Olivia's lips tightened, and she nodded. ''And his wife is home, none the wiser. Men—''

''Don't even say it. I hope you aren't including all of us in that category?''

''I'm not.'' She rubbed her forehead. ''Ah, Clifton, this gets worse and worse.''

''You sound as if you don't want to continue.''

She glanced out the window. ''We have to. As much as I can empathize with the child, that robbery left my children without a father. It left Chandra without a father. And I don't know how many more. Eight men died. I can't just walk away like it was all okay because he needed the money to pay for his deceit. The price was too high, even though his daughter was ill."

Clifton reached for her hand. "I'm with you to the end, baby."

She smiled at him briefly and shook her head. "So many people have to pay. I haven't even mentioned his wife, his children in Maryland. How can people do this to each other?" she asked. She filled her cup with coffee and wrapped her hand around the cup for warmth.

It wasn't a question for Clifton to answer. He thought of the first time he met Cooper. The man had played soccer with his daughter in the front yard, looking like the perfect, American middle-class father, living in the perfect, middle-class, suburban neighborhood.

"I still don't know why Joe was killed. I need to know so I can put it behind me."

He took her hand in his. "Before it's all over, you'll know everything." He hadn't told her about Warren Jones's confession to his brother about the hit-and-run killing of Joe. The information was just enough to worry her without any real solution. "He could have recognized something or someone. He could have seen Cooper with one of the robbers and remembered later."

"Then there's Ray. Sally said her husband called his name just before they took him to surgery. I still don't know what she could have meant by that." She sighed. "What now?" She unbuttoned her coat and turned off the blower.

"We'll call Bill to check out Hooper's name on that account. We still haven't proven that he stole the gold, so we'll follow him tomorrow. We'll also check bank accounts under Hooper's name."

"Such slow progress. I feel as if we've worked on this case forever."

"We've made real progress. The funds for the Mayo Clinic more than likely were funneled from an account in Canada, which was probably funneled from the off-shore account. That's a trail that can be followed."

Clifton called Bill from the cell phone and informed him of the daughter. Then he called Canadian information for the number of the Mountain Magic.

It seemed the place was a posh home for the wealthy where the patients received plenty of individualized treatment much better than that offered by the Canadian health care system.

Returning to Vanceboro, they drove to Cooper's cabin on Spednic Lake. Some of the cabins around it were closed for the winter, and they were spaced unevenly around the lake with plenty of space for privacy. People lived in a few, and others still spent the occasional weekend until winter set in with a vengeance.

Cooper's was small, with three bedrooms and an outhouse in back.

"I'd hate to go in there on a subzero morning." Olivia wrinkled her nose.

The biting wind coming from Canada was crisp and sharp that afternoon.

They made their way back to Bangor and checked into the Holiday Inn near the airport.

Once they'd settled in, Clifton called the Hertz Car Rental, pretending to be Hooper, to see what kind of car was available under his name. He hadn't rented a car there. It took three more tries before they found the rental company he'd used under the Hooper alias.

After unpacking, they ate dinner at an out-of-the-way restaurant boasting fresh salmon as their specialty, and then toured the area.

When they returned to their room the light was blinking on the phone. Clifton dialed the number for the recording. Bill requested that Clifton call him immediately.

He dialed Bill's home, since it was well past office hours. Bill picked it up after the first ring. "Someone tried to murder Chandra last night," he announced without preamble.

Clifton sank to the edge of the king-size bed. "How?" he asked. Damnit, he shouldn't have believed her lies about blackmailing somebody else.

"She was strangled with a stocking and thrown over an embankment—close to a similar MO from a month ago, except some minute details are different."

"Have they arrested anyone?" Clifton asked, glancing toward the bathroom when he heard Olivia cheerfully humming some song off-key. He was glad that she was in the bathroom, and couldn't hear.

"They questioned Wheeler, but let him go. They didn't have enough evidence to hold him. Seems she blackmailed him. The letter was found on her car seat."

"The money?"

"Gone. Though he claimed he paid her the five thousand the previous night."

Clifton swore, ripely. "How is she?"

"She's in a coma. It's critical. I don't think they expect her to survive."

He swore again. "Keep me posted," he said, and disconnected. He punched a fist in the pillow. So damn hardheaded.

The bathroom door opened. Olivia appeared, dressed in a skimpy aqua nightgown. Though it reached her calf, its V-neck veered past her breasts, and the back was all but nonexistent.

Darn, she looked exquisite. But Clifton forced his mind to the sad business at hand.

"Come here," he said, patting the bed beside him. With a graceful stride, she crossed the room, a secret smile cloaking her, her delicious aroma reaching him as she neared. She sat in the space close to him.

Clifton lifted a hand, caressed her cheek. He took her hand in his, her rose-colored polish flawless on her neatly filed fingernails.

He told her the unpleasant, heartrending news.

First thing the next morning, Olivia called Bill for a progress report on Chandra. She was still in a coma, but she was holding on. A policeman was stationed at her door for protection.

Olivia clung to that small hope. Clifton was outside, packing the luggage in the car.

Cooper's plane was due to land in two hours, and she called the airport to make sure his flight was arriving on schedule.

It was.

Giving him time to land and get to the car rental agency, they waited for him to pick up his car and followed him. He traveled the same stretch through logging country they'd used the previous day. From the roadway only thick pines were to be seen, but if a person were to stop and walk a few feet back, they'd see nothing but clear acreage. Not all logging companies replanted after they cleared the area of trees. What a waste.

First he made a supermarket stop—the same supermarket Clifton and Olivia had used—then he drove to his cabin and started a fire. He unloaded his luggage and groceries. Soon smoke billowed from the chimney.

They were in for a very long wait.

"Cooper could have tried to kill Chandra," Olivia finally said. She'd fought bouts of tears and self-blame for the young woman's situation. It had been in the wee hours of the morning before either of them slept.

"Umm." Clifton rubbed the bridge of his nose. "I keep thinking of the letter he and his wife argued over." *Could it have been the blackmail letter?* he wondered.

Olivia tightened her jaw. "If he's the one, he can't get away with this a second time."

"He won't." *Why hadn't Chandra listened to him?*

Clifton noticed that the houses near them were vacant. Just before dark settled completely, he went to an outhouse near where they'd parked. He was surprised to see a double-seat toilet in the single building. He shook his head as the distinct odor emerged. Who would want to share?

Olivia made the trip after him. "We're going to have to do better than this in the future," she said as she poured antibacterial hand gel into her hand and rubbed it in.

"You're the one who wanted a taste of an investigator's life. It isn't all fun, lady."

"I don't know. We've had some good moments." It was too dark for him to see her mischievous grin, but he definitely heard it.

Clifton glanced at the house. Cooper looked as if he'd settled in for the night. The light had disappeared fifteen minutes ago.

Clifton turned up the armrest, leaned toward Olivia, and pulled her into his arms.

"I haven't made love in a car since I was a teenager," he said between kisses.

"I've never done it, ever."

"Then it's about time you lived the experience," he said, peeling off her jacket.

After they cleared the steam from the windows, Clifton and Olivia slept in shifts. It was almost midnight when Cooper dampened the fire and returned to the car. Only a few vehicles passed this stretch of road.

A short delay for the border check, and he continued on. Clifton and Olivia did the same—not wanting too much distance to separate them—enough so he couldn't tell they were tailing him. They were pretty certain of his destination.

The twisting road was dark and long. Clifton glanced at his rearview mirror. It must be his paranoid tendency, he thought, that sent a shiver up his spine. He'd been sweating bullets since he got off the plane in Bangor. Without his gun he felt as naked as a jaybird—definitely vulnerable. PI licenses were only valid in the state they were issued. Clifton didn't have a license to carry a weapon in Maine. He regarded the dark forest, climbing like mountains on each side of him. The car drove slowly behind him all the way to Frederickton. But when Cooper turned off the main road, Clifton didn't follow him. He passed two turns before veering left. The car behind him continued on, the taillights disappearing around a curve by the time Clifton completed a U-turn. Clifton still didn't expel a sigh of relief.

Minutes later, he pulled in front of Mary's house. The street was quiet and dark.

Although they were pretty certain of the facts, Clifton wanted pictures of Cooper with Mary before turning it all over to the police and the insurance company. Clifton used his night-vision camera to snap pictures of him entering the house with his own key, carrying a suitcase. It was one thing to say the man had an offshore bank account. But when information was illegally gained, one couldn't actually use the straightforward method. Once the information was gathered, a detective had to then find the motivation and proof—motivation in this case being a child who needed special care in an expensive clinic. If he'd tried to murder Chandra, the motivation was more than likely blackmail.

They wedged their rented car between two parked cars, half hidden by overhanging branches, to hide their Maine license plates, which would stick out like a sore thumb.

At 8:00 A.M. Clifton took pictures of the couple exiting the house, holding hands. Cooper opened the car door for Mary, and leaned down to kiss her before closing it.

Could he actually try to murder someone one day, and go on as if nothing had happened less than forty-eight hours later?

Sure he could.

"I bet he doesn't do that with his wife," Olivia scoffed, glaring at him. "Probably doesn't even open the door for her any longer."

"I don't know if involving you in detective business is a good idea."

"Makes you think twice about marriage. That's for sure." Underneath the small talk was a burning sensation clinging to Olivia's gut. To this man, he was on just another vacation. His wife was in Maryland, out of sight, out of mind. The eight people murdered twelve years ago, out of sight, out of mind. He just kissed his girlfriend and began his vacation. Perhaps he had even hurt Chandra.

He merged into the traffic and drove half an hour, passing quiet towns until they turned on a quiet street with winding, twisting curves. Another mile and the car stopped at a private, guarded, ornate gate—to

Mountain Magic. As Clifton drove by slowly, Olivia
took pictures of the car at the gate, with Clifton giving
her detailed instructions.

Soon after, the gate opened to admit them.

Clifton and Olivia parked beside the road behind
a car several yards past the entrance to the estate.

"As thirsty as I am, I guess I shouldn't drink anything right now."

"Unless you like squatting by the bushes," Clifton
offered, helpfully.

She threw him a jaundiced look.

Clifton held up his hands. "Just kidding, sweetheart."

Olivia regarded him, a softness stealing her breath
at his wicked behavior. It had been a long time since
someone called her sweetheart. She liked the sweet
names he called her. She thought of their lovemaking
last night—in the car. Who would have believed that
she'd do such a thing? If she ever heard of her children making out in a backseat, she'd give them a
stern lecture that would ring in their ears for months.
Yet there she'd been, steaming up the windows with
Clifton.

Her ruminations were cut short when Cooper's car
reappeared. She'd thought the couple would make
a day of it at the clinic, but they'd stayed less than
fifteen minutes.

This time a bouncy, blond, teenage girl sat in the
backseat.

A car passed and Clifton pulled out behind it, putting some distance between them and Cooper. They
drove for fifteen minutes and stopped at a restaurant.
When the trio exited their vehicle and went in, Clifton

spotted a McDonald's across the street and pulled into the yard.

"If you have to make a pit stop, now is the time. If you hear the horn, hurry back," he told Olivia.

Grabbing a large cosmetic bag, Olivia hurried out of the car and rushed to use the rest room, quickly washing her face and underarms and brushing her teeth. Then she ran back. Glancing out the window, she saw that the car was still in the restaurant yard. She went to the counter and ordered two large coffees and French fries. She had sandwiches in the car.

Clifton opened his door when she returned, a small shaving bag in hand.

"Get two more large coffees. I'm pouring this in the thermos for later. I'll fix sandwiches for us," she told him. While he was gone, she made two hoagies from the sandwich fixings in the cooler, all the while keeping a careful eye on the car across the street.

When Clifton returned, he moved the car to the edge of the lot. They ate their sandwiches, drank coffee, and made small talk.

In an hour, the trio left the restaurant. Anyone observing would assume they were watching a normal family on an outing for the day.

Clifton and Olivia followed the trio to a shopping mall, Odell Park, and Arboretum. He and Olivia stretched their legs as they followed the group on a walk in Mactaquac Provincial Park, monitoring them from a safe distance. Clifton clasped her hand as they traversed nature trails. They went across a bridge that crossed a large beaver pond. At one point, trying to playfully evade his daughter, Cooper fell across a bush.

Later that afternoon, they followed the group back to the house.

While Cooper played with his daughter, Clifton glimpsed a bandage on his arm. He must have hurt himself in the park.

Olivia and Clifton spent another night in the uncomfortable car. Each alternated sleep. They made one trip to the gas station rest room two hours after the couple arrived. Locking the door, each had the privacy to wash before proceeding to their vigil.

By late the next day, it seemed Cooper was in Canada for the week.

"Do you like lobster?" Clifton asked. They needed a break from the tension.

"Love it, but I'd love a bath even more." Olivia had never felt so grungy.

"Let's spend the night in Eastport. Take a trip to a salmon farm and let them pack some on dry ice for the trip back." He yawned. "We can pick it up in the morning on our way to the airport."

"Do you want me to drive?"

He shook his head. "I'm fine."

They drove straight to Eastport, Clifton vigilant for any car that may be following them. He detected nothing unusual along the way.

A quaint B&B on Moose Island, just a short walk from the waterfront, and with private baths, was too irresistible to pass up. The Victorian home was built in the mid 1800's. Once established in their second-floor bedroom decorated with Victorian furniture, they changed their plane reservations to the next afternoon and called Bill. Bill had called the offshore bank, complaining that the funds for Mountain Magic were unavailable. The bank assured him that the funds had cleared, as usual, that there must be some error.

They made a mad dash for the clawfoot tub, and since neither wanted the other to go first, they shared. Reclining at either end, they soaked.

"Now that you have me here, I'm never leaving." Submerged in bubbles up to her chin, Olivia closed her eyes.

"Don't give me any ideas. It's too small, and I'm too old for naughty games."

"And I thought I'd hooked up with a man with imagination who knew how to improvise—at the least take advantage of every occasion." Olivia ran her toes along his thigh, the water lapping at her breasts. Her foot brushed against him intimately. She felt the pulse.

"If you're not awake, something else is," she teased.

"Lady, you're asking for it." His soapy hand snaked up her inner thigh.

His eyes narrowed to slits as he stroked every inch of her body, the soap and water making his caress smooth and soft, like little feathers dancing over her body.

His muscles bunched under Olivia's gentle stroke, the contrast of fingertips and nails gently dragging over his hot skin.

When they came together, water sloshed over the rim in rhythm with the motion of their bodies. And when the pulsating came to a halt, they clung to each other.

Later, only the cooling water and goosebumps on their skin drew them apart.

"Do you think they heard us downstairs?" Olivia asked, stepping on the rug beside the tub.

Clifton glanced over the rim. "If they didn't, they're probably mopping up, at least."

It was another hour before they fell asleep in each other's arms in the hotel's feathery four-poster bed.

They slept three hours, dressed, and opted for dinner at the Fresh Catch Restaurant, where the owner purchased fresh seafood every morning that had barely finished kicking. When they left the restaurant, just enough daylight was left for a walk along the shore. The small town was a showplace of nineteenth-century homes.

After days of living in the confines of a car, the walk was marvelous. It wasn't the brisk pace she usually took, but a leisurely stroll, hand-in-hand. As they made their way along Water Street, twenty-five-foot tides battered the pink granite breakwater. A more awesome sight she'd yet to see. The wind off the Channel buffeted them. Pleasure cruises were replaced with scallop drags and fishing boats.

Their walk carried them to Estes Head, a breathtaking climb through spruce, birch, maples, elm trees, and various bushes. Suddenly Olivia stopped.

"Look at these berries." Red fireballs hung from some branches. The dazzling scarlet was so significant that the orange and yellow balls were uninspiring in comparison. If the inn's owner hadn't mentioned the berries to them, they wouldn't know they were blueberries.

They continued the climb, cresting at a sheer ledge

that dropped to the water. Clifton wrapped an arm around her as they enjoyed the magnificent view, spoiled only by the chill skipping along his spine. He glanced around, dragging Olivia away from the cliff.

Olivia sighed, wishing she could spend a week there with Clifton, without a worry, with the sole purpose of enjoyment.

"Do we have to go back?" she entreated.

"We have to turn the information over to the insurance company and Ben Williams, and he'll take it from there." He nuzzled her neck, nudged her toward the walk back.

"Not the FBI?"

"Solving that case will be a real feather in Ben's cap. It was his former partner's help that gave us the information we needed."

"I just wish I could talk to Cooper," she said, almost losing her footing on the rocky slope.

He squeezed her hand, wrapped an arm around her waist, and drew her close. "You will, after the arrest. But if we approach him now, he'll run. You don't want that."

"No." They had reached the hotel, and the sun was setting. They sat on a bench out front in the cold, wrapped arm in arm, and watched the red reflection on the water. When the fire disappeared, they entered the inn and shared sherry with the innkeeper and other guests in front of the fireplace, where blazing flames licked and swayed.

One couple was from New York, the other from Wisconsin.

When Clifton and Olivia climbed the stairs, fresh

flowers brightened their room, and bedside chocolates satisfied their sweet tooth.

Olivia and Clifton had made love for the first time
mere days ago. Now, they were in the shower together,
bathing for the second time that day. He used his
hands to rub soap over her body. It was a testimonial
to Clifton's gentle regard that she relaxed enough to
even let him see her unclothed.

Olivia loved the complexity of his touch, which at
one moment could be as gentle as a feather, the next,
urgent and demanding.

From the shower, they went to the bedroom. Olivia
took a sheet from her suitcase and covered the spread.
She urged Clifton to lie on his back, his head at the
foot of the bed. She knelt at his head, where he
wrapped his arms around her back. Her thin red silk
nightgown offered no protection against his touch—
his warmth.

"You can't relax like this," she said, but didn't try
to wriggle away.

"I don't want to relax." He stroked from her neck
to her behind—wherever he could reach. "I want
you." His husky voice bought goose pimples on her
arms, but she was determined to finish the massage.
She started to moan.

"You're going to love this," she promised.

With a kiss, he let her go.

Using her fingertips, she used a circular motion on
his head and watched him relax by degrees.

She poured a sweet, almond oil blend in her hands,

rubbing them together to warm the oil before brushing a light film on his skin. Starting on his neck, she used a delicate stroke, then worked her way to his chest. Her movements were slow and long.

Clifton closed his eyes as she maneuvered her way down his body, taking her time, letting him enjoy, until it was time to flip him onto his stomach. Starting at the neck again, she proceeded down one side of his back, alternating efflurage strokes and kneading, then administered to his other side.

By now, she sensed he'd relaxed into a dream state, and she continued, massaging him from head to toe.

When Olivia had finished she returned to his back and sides, but changed her strokes to sensual caresses.

Leisurely, Clifton turned over and pulled her to him, kissing her deeply.

"Woman, I can't move." But he managed to flip her on the mattress and stroke her all over, leaving no detail ignored. When they finally came together, the experience was tumultuous.

Clifton got the best night's sleep he'd had in years.

They drove to the salmon farm and purchased salmon early the next morning. They had a few hours before their flight departed. They took one last stroll along the town, where hearty seagulls flew along the water.

"We'll return one day," Clifton promised. He leaned toward her, sealed his vow with a kiss. Putting the car in gear, he drove away from their short vacation in paradise.

* * *

Half an hour later, while crossing a bridge, a tire blew. Clifton barely missed the embankment. Usually on a blowout, he'd coast to a peaceful stop. This time the car pitched and swayed, halting with no more than a foot to spare.

Chapter 13

They were a couple in love, snuggled together on their plane ride to BWI Airport, but Clifton regarded his surroundings carefully, never letting his guard down for a moment.

After they returned home and unpacked, Olivia drove to the hospital to check on Chandra's progress while Clifton talked to Ben and the insurance company about his findings.

Chandra's mother was just returning from the cafeteria when Olivia intercepted her. Chandra was still in a coma. The women conversed in the young woman's room. The doctor had said it was better for her to hear talking. "She really enjoyed working at the spa," Norma Smith said. "I don't know why she stopped. She even told me you were helping her pick out classes so she could advance."

Chandra's mother appeared no more than forty-five, with a striking resemblance to her daughter. But her nature was more serious, her dress more subdued, in a navy pantsuit with a plain, gold-toned necklace. There was nothing flamboyant or nonsensical about her.

Olivia wondered how she'd paired with Chandra's father. Perhaps the fact that he was her complete opposite had charmed her, but she had been sensible enough to avoid a losing situation. Charm wore off quickly in the light of bills and responsibility.

"She's all I have." Her lips trembled. A tear slid down her cheeks. "I don't know what I'll do if she doesn't pull through," Norma said.

Olivia comforted her. "She'll be okay. She's a very strong-willed young woman." Olivia knew that much was true.

Clifton had spent most of the previous evening and this morning dealing with the police and FBI and fielding calls from the insurance company. It was mid-afternoon before he had a chance to read through his e-mail. Allen had left two favorable messages. One asked about his trip. Clifton had mentioned to Allen the night he'd dined with Catherine that a case was taking him out of town. The next message invited him to Parents' Weekend at the college.

A sudden warmth spread through Clifton.

Allen was beginning to accept him.

Closing his connection, Clifton pushed back from his desk. He strolled across the room, snagging his jacket from the coatrack, and sailed past Veronica.

"I'm gone for the day."

"Shall I expect you at home tonight?"

Clifton glanced at her. "If you see me."

Her laughter followed him out of the office.

Clifton scanned the parking lot as he entered his car. His first stop was the cleaners. He hadn't taken the time to pick up his clothing before he left.

I've seen that white car before, Clifton thought as he placed his clothing in the backseat. He didn't stare, merely got into his car and slowly drove off. He glanced in his rearview mirror. The same car pulled out three cars behind him.

Clifton decided to test his theory and made turns to go to a grocery store located near his office. Parking in a space close to the door, he took a leisurely stroll out of the car and entered the store. Peering through the window as he gathered a basket, he noticed the same white car parking, tail side in, several rows from where he had parked.

Clifton shoved the cart back into place and walked out the opposite door. When he had reached a row away, the driver noticed him, started the car, and accelerated out of the lot. Clifton read the license plate as it merged into the traffic. He stopped, flipped open his pocket notebook, and jotted down the plate number. Then he made his way back to his car. He called the office and asked Veronica to do a plate search on the number.

Who was following him, and why? He thought of Chandra. Had someone been following her, too?

A mild foreboding that had hung over Clifton like a dense cloud intensified. He called Olivia at the spa and warned her not to leave until he arrived. Though he didn't tell her, he wasn't about to leave her alone until his sense of urgency dissipated. First Chandra, then his tire, and now someone was following him. Had he and Olivia been detected in Maine or Canada? Had he spooked Cooper or Wheeler?

His cell phone rang and he picked it up. It was Veronica with the name and number of a rival agency.

Clifton drove directly to the agent's address, but the office was closed. The agency was a one-man affair run by Doug Pohick. He dialed the number and left a message for Pohick to call him. Clifton perused his surroundings to see if the car was in the vicinity. It wasn't.

He called Olivia again, just to be sure she was still at the spa.

As a police officer for twenty years, he'd made lots of enemies. The rival PI could have been hired by Cooper, or any of his other enemies from Cleveland. But he wasn't taking chances with Olivia. He'd stick to her like a tick until this case was over.

Then Clifton considered that he was living at his sister's place. He returned to his office.

Bill stood at Ronnie's desk, his hands in his pockets, laughing at something she said.

"I've got a situation," Clifton said.

"What is it?" Bill asked.

"Somebody's tailing me."

Bill didn't bother to ask him if he were sure. If a good PI picked up on a tail, it was definitely there.

"Who?"

"Doug Pohick. The tire blew out on our rental car

on a curve near a cliff in Maine. I couldn't pinpoint the cause."

"Too many coincidences," Bill said.

"Exactly. I'm going to stick close to Olivia until I can determine what's going on. Bill, I need you to stay close to Ronnie. It would be better if she didn't stay at the house."

"I'm—" Ronnie started.

"You worry about Olivia. I'll take care of Veronica," Bill assured him.

Clifton went home to pack an overnight bag and followed Olivia's car home at seven. He couldn't help glancing across the street. He wondered why Tompkins didn't get treatment for his agoraphobia. It had to be a dismal state of affairs not be able to leave a house. He'd get claustrophobic, himself. He loved feeling the wind and sunshine on his skin.

He parked his car on the other side of Olivia's in the two-car garage and followed her through the inside door that connected to the rec room-turned-bedroom in the basement. They went up the stairs to the main floor.

Olivia dropped her purse on the kitchen table and planted her hands on her hips. "Okay," she said. "Why were you so adamant about following me?"

Clifton's first instinct was to lie to protect her, but Olivia wasn't the kind of woman who'd appreciate rose-colored glasses. She was capable of dealing with the truth. "I caught an investigator following me."

He hands slid down her sides. "How do you know it was an investigator?"

"I checked out his license plate."

"Is anything secret around you people?"

"Not yet. I couldn't catch up with him today, so I don't know why he was following me. I'll just sleep better if I know you're protected."

"And you're just the one to do it."

"Of course," he said, reaching for her. Just the few hours they'd been apart felt like a month.

He captured her lips with his, felt her hands caress his back. He could get used to this.

"You have a lot of tense muscles that need to be worked on," she muttered when they parted. "The other night I merely gave you a Swedish massage, which isn't designed to relax those muscles. Are you up to more tonight?"

Clifton thought of how that night ended, and his body responded immediately. His hardness pressed against her, and he definitely needed her, but he shook his head. "As much as I want to, I can't afford to relax into a deep sleep tonight."

"I guarantee you won't be relaxed. The process may be a bit painful, though."

He nuzzled her neck. "So that's the way you get your kicks."

"There are many facets to me I've yet to disclose," Olivia professed, and urged him toward the stairs.

"I aim to discover every one of them," he promised.

The next day, Chandra moved, flicked an eyelid, and moved her mouth, but didn't come completely out of her coma. She was monitored closely by staff and the police. The insurance company was especially interested, feeling that she might have additional information about the heist. They all but camped out near her room. Clifton found the area secure.

Between the time Olivia and Clifton spent at the hospital, Clifton tried to contact Pohick. The man couldn't be found at his office or his home. There were plenty of places to get lost in the area.

"Do you think he's still following us?" Olivia asked.

Clifton glanced in his rearview mirror. "No. I haven't detected him today."

"Cooper just can't leave well enough alone."

"We don't know it was him. It's just a hunch. Unless it's from an old case of mine back in Cleveland. With Cooper's millions, he can pay for just about anything."

"They won't be his for long."

They made one last stop at Chandra's room before they returned to Olivia's home for the night.

Around 2:00 A.M. Clifton heard movement downstairs. He put a hand across Olivia's mouth and wakened her, whispered to her to lie on the floor in the closet while he went to investigate. He felt the floor beside the bed and pulled his .38 out of the holster. Then he took the four pillows from the bed and arranged them under the covers to resemble two bodies.

Stealthily, he approached the door and leaned against the wall on the left side—away from the line of sight to the bed. He heard a stair creak. In seconds after he was in place a man came into view, stretching a stocking in front of him with both hands.

He must have sensed something wrong, because just as Clifton moved he swirled, dropped the stocking, and kicked out. Clifton evaded the kick, and with two swift movements had the man flat on the floor, cold.

Suddenly Clifton sensed someone behind him and turned just in time to duck a blow to the head. It caught his hand instead, and knocked his gun across the floor. A knife appeared in the man's hand and nicked Clifton's hand before he disarmed the man. He and his opponent fought their way toward the gun.

At the same time, he heard a wild shriek and saw Olivia flying toward them with a baseball bat held over her head. The apparition startled his opponent, giving Clifton time to get in enough licks to finish him off.

Clifton retrieved his gun and clipped handcuffs on both men while Olivia stood guard with her bat. The ringing from her shrieks still sounded in his ears.

"What do you think you were doing?" he finally asked. By now he sounded like a tape recording. Olivia always did the unexpected.

"You were outnumbered," she said, eyes wide with fear.

He wanted to go to her, to erase that fear. She wasn't accustomed to violence. He hoped to calm her as much as possible. He shook his head in resignation. "With you around?"

"I'll call the police," she said, carrying her bat with her to the phone.

"Hold off a couple of minutes, will you?"

She stopped, her hand over the receiver. "What? We can't let them go."

"I don't intend to. I've got a few questions I need answers to before the police get here."

Olivia hovered near the phone and nodded.

"Honey, why don't you go downstairs and get me a drink of water? I'm thirsty. But don't hurry."

"I can't leave you up here alone with them. Something may happen."

He intended for something to happen. She didn't need to know that. "I'll be fine. They can't get away."

She left the room, still carrying her bat.

Clifton regarded the men. "Now, who hired you?" he asked.

Olivia didn't get the opportunity to talk to Cooper. But the man who murdered her husband was one of the two who were sent after Clifton and her, hired by none other than Cooper.

It seems Joe had remembered that Mary brought her child into the office the previous month in a tear because Cooper hadn't been sending the support money for her treatments at Mountain Magic. Joe and Lawrence had overheard part of the conversation.

Cooper had picked up the line in the office when Joe had called Nelson, the detective in charge of the case.

"Not everyone would have agreed to split that money among the families the way you did," Clifton said more than a month later.

"We all lost someone special in that robbery. They all need it more than I do," Olivia said.

Clifton shook his head. Her generosity amazed him. None of them had received the money yet, but Olivia's instructions to the insurance company were to have it split among the families of the eight men who died—and also with him.

Chandra's mother would get her share, which would pay for her daughter's counseling and her college degree. Physically she was on the mend. She had moved back in with her mother, and was still recuperating. With luck, the counseling would help her deal with her father's death. She had even signed up to attend Howard University the second semester. She had a very promising future ahead of her.

Every day, it seemed, something new surfaced. U.S. and Canadian Immigration, the Canadian Mounties, and the FBI had worked to get Cooper back to the States. They had uncovered ten million so far in the offshore accounts, and had promising leads. They were still searching for the rest.

It was Thanksgiving weekend. Allen, Craig, and Rochelle were at the movies. Ronnie and Bill had disappeared.

After stuffing themselves on the turkey dinner at Olivia's house, Olivia and Clifton opted for a hike.

The wind was brisk, and they'd worn several layers of clothing to keep warm.

Clifton held her gloved hand as they strolled along the grassy bank of the Potomac.

"Allen has really come around," Olivia said.

Clifton smiled, remembering how his son had thrown an arm around his shoulder Wednesday night in a roughhouse greeting. "He has."

Hearty winter birds flocked above them. Suddenly, Clifton stopped. "The Total Woman only provides services for women?"

"That's right," Olivia said, urging him to quicken his pace. This had started out as a brisk walk.

He wouldn't be budged. "So that means I'm going to have to marry you to get regular massages?"

Olivia sucked in a cold breath. *Marry her?*

He started walking again, forcing her into motion. After a hundred feet Clifton said, "I'm waiting."

She unglued her tongue from the roof of her mouth. "That's right," she whispered.

"Is that a yes?"

Olivia nodded. In another moment, she was in his arms.

Epilogue

Olivia and Clifton stood on the shores of the St. John in New Brunswick. It was June, and the temperature was a vast improvement over what it had been in October. Olivia sighed dreamily. They were on yet another honeymoon. Clifton looked for any excuse to take honeymoons. They'd taken a cruise after they married, during college spring break in March.

Now they were taking a two-week vacation in several locales in New Brunswick, Nova Scotia, and Maine.

Clifton was between cases, and Rochelle was working in the Spa while Olivia was away. Bill and Veronica were still pretending they weren't attracted to each other.

Olivia had lost another ten pounds. She and Clifton worked out together almost daily now. She wasn't up to jogging, but she did do a fast walk now. Exercising with Clifton made the experience another adventure instead of a hated necessity.

Olivia was complete and satisfied within herself, but marriage had added a new dimension. Now, she took more time just to enjoy life.

Clifton had worried that he would be as inattentive with her as he'd been to his first wife. He needn't have worried at all.

As they trekked up a hill, Olivia was glad of the exercise. Clifton wasn't one to relax at a time share for a week. This man had them moving from place to place, and tried to walk every square inch of each locale. Six months ago, Olivia couldn't have kept up.

Now she could.

Olivia realized she may never lose all the weight, but Clifton loved her anyway. The important issue was that with exercise, she felt better.

Dear Reader:

I hope you enjoyed the time you spent with Olivia and Clifton in *Tender Escape*. I had so much pleasure writing about a nontypical heroine.

All women should be cherished, whatever their size, for they are so much more. They nurture everyone (many times to the exclusion of themselves)—children, husbands, parents, friends, communities. When we only look at size, we miss the true spirit beneath.

In the meantime, I'm working on my next book, *Shattered Illusions,* set in southern Virginia. It is scheduled for release in November 2000.

Thank you for so many kind and uplifting letters, and for your support.

I love hearing from readers. You may write to me at:

P.O. Box 291
Springfield, VA 22150

With Warm Regards,
Candice Poarch

ABOUT THE AUTHOR

Reared in a small town in Southern Virginia, best-selling author Candice Poarch portrays a sense of community and mutual support in her novels. She firmly believes that everyday life in small-town America has its own rich rewards.

Candice currently lives in Springfield, Virginia with her husband of twenty-two years and three children. A former computer systems manager, she has made writing her full-time career. Candice is a graduate of Virginia State University and holds a Bachelor of Science degree in physics.

BOOK YOUR PLACE ON OUR WEBSITE AND MAKE THE ARABESQUE ROMANCE CONNECTION!

We've created a customized website just for our very special Arabesque readers, where you can get the inside scoop on everything that's going on with Arabesque romance novels.

When you come online, you'll have the exciting opportunity to:

- View covers of upcoming books

- Learn about our future publishing schedule (listed by publication month and author)

- Find out when your favorite authors will be visiting a city near you

- Search for and order backlist books

- Check out author bios and background information

- Send e-mail to your favorite authors

- Join us in weekly chats with authors, readers and other guests

- Get writing guidelines

- AND MUCH MORE!

Visit our website at
http://www.arabesquebooks.com

More Sizzling Romance from
Candice Poarch

Coming in March from Arabesque Books . . .

FORBIDDEN HEART by Felicia Mason
1-58314-050-6   **$5.99**US/**$7.99**CAN

When savvy Mallory Heart needs someone to oversee construction of her first boutique, she turns to Ellis Carson. Although he has little in common with the college-educated men she's used to and he thinks she's a snob, soon enough they start concentrating on their shared interest in each other.

PRECIOUS HEART by Doris Johnson
1-58314-083-2   **$5.99**US/**$7.99**CAN

Burned by love, Diamond Drew is determined never to trust another man again. But after meeting handsome Dr. Steven Rumford, everything changes. Since he comes with a disastrous past as well, the couple must learn to trust each other if they can ever hope to find happiness together.

A BITTERSWEET LOVE by Janice Sims
1-58314-084-0   **$5.99**US/**$7.99**CAN

When Teddy Riley secures an interview with reclusive author Joachim West, she never expects that a freak accident will lead to her being mistaken for his wife . . . or that she might find an irresistible passion that promises a future filled with a joyful, healing love.

MASQUERADE by Crystal Wilson-Harris
1-58314-101-4   **$5.99**US/**$7.99**CAN

Offered a chance to housesit in Miami, Madison Greer soon meets Clint Santiago, the most handsome, mysterious man she's ever encountered. But Clint is really a federal agent trying to bust a drug dealer and to do that, he'll have to get close to Madison and risk losing his heart forever . . .

Please Use the Coupon on the Next Page to Order

Ring in the Spring
with Arabesque Books

__**FORBIDDEN HEART by Felicia Mason**
  1-58314-050-6   **$5.99**US/**$7.99**CAN

__**PRECIOUS HEART by Doris Johnson**
  1-58314-083-2   **$5.99**US/**$7.99**CAN

__**A BITTERSWEET LOVE by Janice Sims**
  1-58314-084-0   **$5.99**US/**$7.99**CAN

__**MASQUERADE by Crystal Wilson-Harris**
  1-58314-101-4   **$5.99**US/**$7.99**CAN
